THE PEARLMAKERS

THE HUNT FOR LA GRACIA

DUKE TATE

ISBN 978-1-951465-29-2 print
ISBN 978-1-951465-30-8 MOBI
ISBN 978-1-951465-31-5 EPUB

Cover design by Emily's World of Design

Pearl Press, LLC
PO Box 2036
Del Ray Beach, Florida
33483

CONTENTS

Deep in the sea are riches beyond compare.
But if you seek safety, it is on the shore.

— SAADI (ROSE GARDEN)

1

Teddy Dollarhide's eyes sprang open as he jackknifed awake on the outside porch sofa. Beads of sweat dotted the back of his neck and he squinted through the glare of the sun. He looked around for his crew and the ocean, but only saw a pasture and a barn off to his right. Then he realized that he was safely at home and it was all a dream—but not just any dream. It was the same dream he had been having for the last fifteen years about being a crewmember on a massive Spanish galleon on its way down in a violent hurricane. He could still hear the wind, feel the adrenaline, taste the saltwater on his tongue.

Maybe one day I'll get used to it, he thought. *One day.*

Shaking the dream off, he went inside to draw the dream, a compulsion he had maintained since they started. He was a big, wide, barrel-chested man who attributed his strength to growing up on a farm and to years of sport fishing. Friends called him "Old Salt," and with his pearl hair, matching beard, and ruddy skin, the title suited him.

After scribbling down a new sketch, he went back outside to relax on the stone porch. Gazing out over the land, he reflected on the dreams, thinking back to when they started. He had been a history professor at the University of Miami when they started coming in the night, once every two months, then once a month, and eventually once or twice a week. Over the years, he couch-surfed from psychiatrist to psychiatrist and from therapist to therapist to unravel the connection between himself and the sailor haunting him, but it didn't help, and the pharmacopeia and half-wit they threw at him only turned the dreams into nightmares. Charcoal stained the tips of his fingers from his ongoing drawings of the dream, which covered the walls of his home office in Miami. Stacks of books on treasure and Spanish galleons towered to the ceiling and stuffed the interior. But in all the pages of the books, he couldn't find anything resembling the ship from his dreams and he had resigned to it being nothing more than a figment of his unconscious imagination.

One day while drawing, he got a call informing him that a distant uncle had passed and bequeathed him an Italian Mediterranean-style estate named "Isabella" that sat only 150 meters off the ocean on over sixty acres in a little town called Latchawatchee, Florida. A real estate investor, Red Dollarhide had bought the rundown mansion years ago at a killer price with plans to chop up and sell off the land. Teddy inherited the property tax and maintenance to go with the twenty million dollar estate, which was a burden considering the fact that Red had only left him a half a million in trust besides the property, having squandered his money on bad deals.

When Teddy and his wife, Sarah, were given the keys to Isabella, they were certain their plan was simply to sell it off —netting enough to settle the obligations and pocket a nice sum for themselves—but one step through the ten-foot-tall mahogany door changed everything. Netted cobwebs blocked doorways, dust caked the floors, the paint was peeling off the walls, mold blackened the ceilings, ants scaled the living room walls, and furniture hid its neglect under drop cloths. But underneath it all, the house exuded the same irresistible charm that had kept Red from selling it over all those years. And their boys, Joey and Cosby, enjoyed playing on the majestic grounds of the estate.

Sarah and Teddy couldn't let go of the house, no matter what it was worth. They spoke about cutting up and selling the land, but even that felt sacred to them. So, they kept the estate intact and did their best to make the property tax payments. Teddy made the repairs himself during their vacations there, while Sarah tended the garden, which she loved since she owned a bespoke landscape architecture business in Coconut Grove. Giving back was also a large priority of hers and she spent months every year in Africa assisting the hungry in obtaining food.

Teddy had just turned thirty-eight and Sarah was two years younger when they first visited Latch to see Isabella. Back then, they thought they were dreaming. In Miami, Teddy had started keeping a loaded gun in his bedside table ever since their house had been robbed. Latch seemed idyllic by comparison. The center of town, laid out in a square, sat a half-mile from the ocean. The Hub, as locals called it, housed a variety of small businesses and restaurants; a 1920s white-washed Spanish courthouse marked the center. A statue of Ponce de León stood in front of the building as a nod to its Spanish roots, which ran deep and wide like the oak trees that dotted the greens. Giant palms lined the streets, and flowers were replaced as soon as they wilted with the turning seasons. Traffic speeds averaged five miles under the posted limit, and children rode their bicycles in the street. A neighborhood of bungalows with wide sweeping porches surrounded the square. The grandest historic homes dotted the small bay along Route 1, which trailed out of town following the ocean north and south. In the summer, the essence of jasmine and honeysuckle filled the dense, steaming air.

On their visits, they would read the crime reports in the town's newspaper, *The Grapevine*, for a good chuckle. One week's highlights included an old lady who called the police after witnessing her neighbor drop an anonymous love letter in her mailbox and a man who had his wallet stolen by a raccoon that snuck in through his dog door.

Due to the sense of safety at Isabella, Teddy slept more hours and got better quality of sleep there. This also meant that his dreams were always more vivid; he sensed that just by being in the area, he might receive a midnight clue to their purpose.

In Miami, the dreams had begun to interfere with his teaching. He and Sarah would often take the boys sailing at Key Biscayne on the weekends, and his mind always felt the clearest on the water; he began to crave its company like a long-lost friend.

They drove up the coast to Isabella at least once a month and Sarah would always cry when they left because she never wanted to leave. One cold October Sunday, she was sobbing as Teddy turned the truck onto Route 1 and a platoon of a hundred seagulls flew up the coast in a cloud of flapping intent. The sight so astonished him that he stopped the truck and, without saying a word, slipped out to watch as the gulls began a circular ballet high above the grey sea. The dance seemed to be communicating something to him. The position of their bodies was forming a symbol, but he couldn't decode it, and then, they all stopped beating their wings for a single moment and he caught a glimpse of meaning. A second later, they flew off just as fast as they had come. Having seen Teddy draw it a thousand times, Sarah confirmed that the birds' pattern was indeed the circle with the cross and lion's head at the top from the admiral's jacket on the ship in his dream.

He took it as a sign and reluctantly quit his teaching job, bought a big boat for treasure hunting that he named *Gold Lip*, and although he was terrified of lacking employment in the face of Isabella's upkeep, decided to start a small inshore fishing business in Latch and move the family there. Sarah relocated her landscaping business as well.

The original structure of Isabella was built in the 17 th century and added onto gradually over the years with a full scale make over in the Italian Mediterranean style during the 1920's. Her exterior walls were white stucco over masonry and every window and door opening was framed in coquina stone quarried in Miami's Coconut Grove. With her tower, she appeared to be an old villa in Capri, Italy.

The roof had the original barrel-shaped clay tiles that were handmade by forming them over the workers' thighs. Isabella had large stone-columned loggias on the front and the back. The 15' tall ceilings ran throughout the first floor and the ceilings in each room had either pecky cypress beams, pecky cypress paneled ceilings, or decorative plaster. Arched openings abounded from one room to the next in long enfilades while giant carved coquina stone mantles graced the living and dining rooms. Pecky cypress mantles were in the sunroom, kitchen and breakfast room. A grand wooden stair in the large foyer ascended to the second floor with its 12' ceilings in each room. Another wooden stair snaked its way from the second floor's long landing up to

the tower, which had 360° views to the ocean and the coun-
tryside over the small town's rooftops.

There was a large indoor tile pool on the back of the
house off the North wing that was very unusual for its
day-and-age.

Isabella was a grand lady with the air of an Italian movie
star like Sophia Loren–noble but earthly, with something of
both the peasant and the aristocrat in her soul. Teddy and
his family loved living in her, and she loved them back. She
warmed them when they were cold, cooled them when they
were hot, sheltered them from the rain and ocean winds,
and her spirit lifted them up from the earth in which she
stood. The land had a way of consoling their pain and
enhancing their dreams. While shuffling through some
books in the two-story library one day, Teddy stumbled
upon a gold-leafed, out-of-print hardback about treasure
ships in Florida; one ship in particular struck a chord with
him. A Spanish galleon named *La Gracia* had been caught in
a hurricane off the coast of northeast Florida in the seventeenth century and sank while carrying enormous quanti-
ties of gold, silver, and jewels. Hunters had searched for it
but never found any trace—in fact, many had concluded
that it was just a smoke ship and the stories were mere
legends. The name and description rang true in the core of
Teddy's being, and he knew it was the very ship he had been
dreaming about. He googled it and found a little more
history. One line made his mouth drop: "The ship went
down off the coast of a little town called Latchawatchee."

The revelation floored Teddy and Sarah. They popped a
bottle of champagne and, after a few glasses, chased each
other around the house, laughing. And Teddy continued to
fish the waters where *La Gracia* fell, hoping that the seagulls
would return with further instructions.

Meanwhile, Sarah and Teddy loved many aspects of living in Latch, but came to learn that it really was frozen in time. In an attempt to preserve the pleasantries of a slower, quieter era, the town had resisted change. When it landed on a certain travel magazine's list of the top one hundred places to retire, some residents wrote letters of disgust to the editors. Growth in the last ten years had increased housing costs as retirees and snowbirds from northern cities flocked in search of their own private tropical Mayberry. That in turn encouraged aggressive real estate development up and down the virgin Atlantic coastline.

What no one knew when they first moved there was that behind the perfect exterior, Latch had a history that wasn't written about in the pages of the magazines and rarely spoken about among the residents. The town's past covered the area like an invisible cloak of darkness, overtaking anyone who was susceptible to it; some residents gossiped, others were crooked or ignorant, and corruption had spread like a virus to a few key people in charge.

Tongues wagged about Teddy and Sarah to. They lived on modest salaries in one of the grandest houses in the area, and it was rumored that he made paper airplanes out of charity ball invitations, preferring to give a small anonymous amount on his own each month. Although the gossipers were nice to their faces, they loathed Teddy's old truck and his going shirtless around the marina and how Sarah was always bringing guests of a *lower station* over for dinner.

Nevertheless, in time, Teddy's sport fishing business became successful as it was the only one in the area and he could really spin a reel and find the fish—Sarah's land-scaping business boomed, too, as she capitalized on the snowbirds. Their children did well in school and made friends with good people.

Things seemed to be going well until the four-year mark, when Sarah contracted a rare form of bone cancer and died four months later. The second her heart stopped beating in the upstairs tea room, the power went out in Isabella, and for months, the morning dew held onto the windows throughout the day. Teddy was a hollow shell of his former self; only his love for their boys anchored him in his daily life. Without her salary, the property tax on Isabella made finances tight, so Teddy resorted to drawing on even more of Red's trust to make the payments. The dreams increased, and one day at dawn, while going for a walk on the beach, he crossed the dune bridge to find hundreds of his old messengers, the seagulls, covering the sand, staring straight up at him. They squawked and then turned their heads out to the sea. In an instant, they flew off in unison toward the horizon, disappearing into the rising sun. He waited for them to return, but they never did. It was the motivation he had been waiting for to start searching the Atlantic with *Gold Lip* for the treasure of *La Gracia*, hoping to solve his financial woes.

A crew of honest hunters willing to work for a cheap hourly rate and the promise of a future cut of the treasure was hard to find. Teddy called some old buddies from Miami who agreed to join him, and he dubbed them "the Pearlmakers" after his love of oysters. Growing up in the Deep South, he had acquired an insatiable appetite for the shelled delicacies that no man could equal. He also bought an ROV (remotely operated underwater vehicle) for when they searched in deeper waters. In the six years since they had started hunting, they had found many pieces of the galleon, but nothing of significant value.

Propping his bare, calloused feet up on the stone railing of the porch, he leaned his chair back and observed the sky. The wind blew hard, whispering a secret as it curled over his ear: *a change is coming.* He took out his phone and texted the crew with instructions to meet him at the marina the following day at two o'clock. He'd decided to spend the day working in the Dog House, his work shed.

2

Cosby Dollarhide, a blond, curly-headed, lanky but fit high school senior, paddled out for another wave. The previous night's storm brought big breaks, but his partner needed small ones. Dog—his short-legged Jack Russell—stood at the front of the board with his tongue blowing in the wind. Cosby turned into a three-foot wave and rose. As they rode the wave, Dog grinned and wagged. They coasted to the shore, where Dog jumped off into the water and yelped for more.

"No boy, you have to sit the big ones out." Cosby leashed Dog, then tied him to a lifeguard stand before running back into the sea. Dog yapped in a high-pitched voice.

Cos paddled out and ducked under three subpar waves. The hot sun felt good on his skin. Then he saw a wave building that looked like an eight-footer.

He turned, paddled into the wave at an angle, and dropped into the barrel; for a moment, time stopped and he felt one with the ocean, beating with the natural rhythm of the universe. When the tube rolled over him, he held his hand for balance on the inside of the cylindrical curl, which appeared like glass being blown as it moved overhead.

He was short coming out of the chute and the tail knocked him sideways. He took a huge breath before going under. The sack thrust him to the bottom in half a second, where he bashed against the ocean floor. He got caught in the undertow and dragged along the bottom like a ragdoll stuck outside a car door. At the mercy of the wave, he relaxed, knowing that tensing up could cause injury. He reached for the leash, but the force of the water was too strong. His knee scraped against something like loose jagged coral, which felt as sharp as metal. The oxygen in his lungs diminished as the pressure held him down. Feeling it ease for a moment, he reached up and managed to grab the cord attached to the board, which bobbed on the surface like a life preserver. Through the force of the current, he climbed the cord to the glimmer of light at the surface. Grabbing onto his board, he paddled to the shore, hobbled over to Dog, and fell down, fatigued. While catching his breath, the small amount of blood coming from his right knee reminded him of the scrape. Something told him that that "coral" was manmade. He had to know, but didn't want to risk going back out. Years on the water had given him a sixth sense for ocean geography, and he could guess that the area sat ten feet from where the big wave was breaking. If he swam out in between waves, he could dive for it.

The waves broke every few minutes. He waited for one to crash before swimming out and tucking his body down to the bottom, pushing hard. His fingers raked through the sand, coming across a broken sand dollar, but no coral. Not wanting to get caught in the undertow again, he swam back up for more air and a view. No wave yet. Ducking to the floor again, his hand touched something rough like coral, but longer and heavier. He grabbed it and returned to the top. Content with the find, he swam back to shore.

Although the object was covered with barnacles, through the crustacean, he made out an antique long-nosed pistol. He walked over to the restrooms and washed it at the outdoor shower spigot and sat down by Dog, flipping it around in his hands.

"This could be from *La Gracia*, Dog."

Jumping up, he grabbed his board and ran to the street where he'd parked his Cannondale mountain bike—white frame, plastered with stickers. Dog followed. He removed a white bandana from the bike's back saddle bags and wrapped the pistol in it, then placed the bundle in one of the bags.

The partners bicycled up Route 1 going north.

Most people called Cosby "Cosmo," a nickname bestowed on him by his physics teacher Tom Thompkins after he observed that the slack-jawed curly-haired blond was spaced out in class. The name spread like wildfire at school, but he didn't care. An outdoorsman who'd rather be catching a wave than parsing equations, unless it had something to do with the arc of a wave or the angle of an over-hanging rock, he had little patience for numbers. But words, even foreign ones, added up for him, and he'd always aced his humanities classes.

They passed from the ocean to the oak and palm tree tailored park along the bay, turning onto Mangrove Avenue toward downtown. He was eager to show Teddy the gun, but needed to swing by the high school to check on his physics exam grade.

He coasted down the bustling street where cars lined the storefronts and people breezed by on the sidewalks, shopping and eating. The floating aroma of baking dough tugged his belly to the Malt, a vintage polished airstream on the edge of a green space that served breakfast, juices, and smoothies. He parked his bike out front. While leashing Dog to a telephone pole, he noticed a WANTED sign stapled to the front of it:

FERAL HOG TERRORIZING
FARM ANIMALS, PETS, AND PEOPLE
$25,000 REWARD DEAD OR ALIVE
CALL WILL BURNS

Below Will's name was his number; below that was an outlined drawing of a hog's head in a box—saliva seeping around the hog's great-white-like teeth. Cos shook his head in disbelief and smiled. He ripped the flyer down, folded it, and tucked it in his pocket.

At the Malt, he ordered fresh-squeezed orange juice and a bagel to go. Grease sizzled in the background as steam rose from the griddle. The Beach Boy's "The Warmth of the Sun" played on a busted up radio that made everything sound like 1964. Watching Miss Jimmy with her red cheeks smear the rosemary butter on his toasted raisin bagel, he overheard two farmers sitting at a picnic table chirping about Half Ton over their lumberjack specials. One with a long, rough face wearing faded Carhartt overalls claimed it was the biggest living thing he'd ever seen. His friend Bill, who had his name stitched on a patch across the chest of his collared shirt stained with black oil smudges, one-upped him by claiming the beast ran in front of his truck on Dog Pound Road near the Willis Plantation chasing after a cat, and he had to swerve off to the side to miss it. Miss Jimmy handed Cos the food with a wide smile and told him she'd slipped two pieces of bacon in there for

Dog, and then winked. He thanked her and exited. Dog and he ate outside by the telephone pole. An old grey Dodge truck swirled dust up in the air as it passed, and Cos swore he spotted a butterfly riding on the rim of the truck bed. They finished eating and headed toward the high school.

Yesterday was his final day of exams, and today was the last for many other students. He cruised with his surfboard in one hand and dog following his wheels through the royal palm-covered campus onto the long brick porch where grades were posted to a bulletin board. Stopping in front of it, he got off and leaned his board against the wall.

Students received a three-digit ID number to maintain privacy. He'd passed his humanities classes with flying colors, but math and science were his kryptonite, and his physics exam would determine whether he graduated—a B or better, and he was through. Scanning the grades, his stomach knotted at the clusters of Cs and Ds. He breathed a sigh of relief when he saw a B+ by his number.

"Yes! Freedom at last. I am finally done with this damn place!"

Pedaling across campus, he noticed a crowd of faculty and students staring dumbstruck at a Caterpillar crane carrying Betsy, the school mascot, out through the third floor biology window. A square leather band supported her girth under the belly. He stopped at the edge of the crowd, watching with a baffled stare.

"It's not every day you see a flying cow," a squat freshman said in a high-pitched voice.

A slim senior with dirty blonde hair walked over and stopped beside Cos. He kept watching Betsy, but smelled the lavender perfume and knew who was close by. Last month, Leslie broke up with her boyfriend of two years, Buzz Smith, and Cos had been waiting for the right moment to ask her out.

To say Cos disliked Buzz would be a vast understatement. He had no clue where Leslie and Buzz connected; everyone knew Leslie loved the Dave Matthews Band—sang the Beach Boys' "Kiss Me Baby" every morning in the shower—and in her spare time she volunteered for the Sierra Club, an environmental organization founded by preservationist John Muir. Buzz listened to bad music and cut class to dump Rubbermaid trashcans full of water out of windows onto unassuming freshman. The *arm* was the *only* explanation—she'd lost it in a car accident when she was thirteen. Some people would retreat after such a disfiguration, but not Leslie—she decided she was going to be God's gift to the world by charming everyone, and she was, but perhaps on the inside, she needed the protection of a big guy like Buzz to stop the next car if it ever came.

"Hi Cos, what's going on?" She smiled at him and pointed up at the cow with her good arm.

"Hey Leslie. It's Betsy, the school mascot. I can't believe they did this," he said, baffled.

"This is the best senior prank ever," the freshman replied.

"Why are they taking her out the window?" Leslie's friend asked.

"Cows can walk up stairs, but not down. So they brought in the crane," Cos said.

"That's unbelievable," Leslie remarked.

"Poor Betsy," Leslie's friend exclaimed.

"I don't think she knows what's going on," Cos said.

"She does seem kind of clueless," Leslie said, smiling.

"I bet she's terrified," her friend exclaimed.

Betsy lifted her tail and dropped yesterday's dinner to the ground.

They chuckled and the crowd belted out. Dog barked. Leslie noticed him, walked over, and started to pet him. He leaned his head back into her hand.

"Hey Dog, been surfing lately?"

"Yep, we just got done," Cos said.

"I bet you liked that."

"He loves it," Cos said. Dog grinned. "So are you finished with exams?"

"Yes! *Thank God!* I just got out of US History."

"Congratulations! Any summer plans?"

"Oh, not much. I'm going to the everglades in July with the Sierra Club. I'll look for a job here when I get back, maybe at the Honey Bee Farm." She noticed the pistol's nose sticking out of the bandana in the saddlebag. "What's that?"

"I think it's an antique gun I found while surfing today." He picked it up and handed it to her.

"How neat, where did it come from?" She opened the bandana to examine the sea-beaten gun.

"I think it may belong to *La Gracia*, the ship my father has been hunting. Did I ever tell you about that?"

"No—I've heard he was a treasure hunter from people," she said. "You know how everyone in Latch talks." Her hazel eyes fixed on his.

"Oh, I see—they're *talking*."

"No, I didn't mean it like *that*."

"I'm just joking," He smiled and she grinned. "*La Gracia* is a Spanish galleon that sank off the coast here. Dad has been trying to find it for the last six years. The gun is from the ship, probably."

"Well, do you think it's worth any money?" she said, looking it over.

"Probably, I don't know. No, definitely. Probably worth a little. Hey, I am going back to the house to show it to dad. You're welcome to come with me if you want to. He can tell you more about the ship."

"Sure! I'd love to!"

"Great!"

"I'll get my bike. This is so cool," she said, handing him the pistol.

"Thanks." She jetted off while Dog and he waited. Virginia Matthews bounced up behind them.

"Hey Virginia, how's it going?" She walked by, spun, and backpedaled, grinning at him.

"Great, Cos! I only have one more exam left." She thought his question was a flirt and blushed a little. "What's new?" she asked.

"Some guy named Melvin likes you. He calls himself The Melvster. I said I would help him get a date. What'd you think?"

"The Melvster? No way," she said, pointing her finger to her mouth like she was trying to make herself vomit.

"C'mon, give the guy a chance. What's one date, for charity?"

She shook her head while smiling. "One too many," she said and spun forward, bouncing off.

"I told you, Melv, but you wouldn't listen." He shook his head, laughing about his potential imaginary date set up between the heartthrob and Melv—anything to take his attention off Leslie. He watched the crane lower Betsy to the ground. The crowd clapped and cheered in applause; she mooed in celebration.

"*Cosby Dollarhide!*" a voice screeched from behind. He turned and saw Miss Leavers, her starched shirt stuffed into a long dress. "Get that flea bag off this campus right now!"

"Okay."

"Some nerve you have bringing him here! Ten percent of kids are 90 percent of the problem, and *you're* the 10 percent, Cosby! Don't you know what happens to dreamers like you?"

"I hadn't thought about it, really." Sitting on his bike, he put on his sunglasses and stared at her casually.

"They end up broke and alone with no one and nothing, not even a stray cat to keep them company. Now get that rodent out of here!"

He shook his head and began to pedal off. Leslie rode her mountain bike over; together, they cycled off the campus and toward the bay.

"Was Miss Leavers giving you a hard time?"

"Yeah."

"Don't worry, she's like that with everyone. I saw her in a mirror once and she didn't even show a reflection."

"Good thing she can't see how scary she is."

They continued until they reached Route 1, which they followed north along the rugged ocean terrain.

After a while, he challenged her to a race to see who could make it to Orange Street first; it was an ambitious challenge, considering the surfboard. She accepted, and when he yelled "GO," they pedaled hard. Her shining hair flew in the wind as she raced past him on the mountain bike. Cos managed to keep up with her, but she beat him there by a good ten feet.

They turned left onto Orange, heading inland on a white sandy road. Green tropical plants and short trees forested the edges; scattered beach houses of different sizes and colors hid behind the vegetation. Cos saw a *Bateman and Banks Lot for Sale* sign sticking out from a spread of thick jungle and hit his brakes. Across the road ahead, four other new signs had sprung up.

The land around Isabella's sixty acres had been chopped up a few years ago, and countless signs had staked plots in the area, but the poorly designed beach houses were only a minor irritation for the Dollarhides. For three years, Bateman and Banks Realty had been petitioning Teddy to sell Isabella so they could use the acreage to overlap Casablanca, a $150 million condo development. They sent, called, and knocked with offers all the time. Teddy just folded the petitions into paper airplanes and sailed them to the trashcan, but in the last couple of weeks, his bin had become something of a hangar, and the calls were becoming more pressing, almost aggressive.

"Damn it, new signs!" Cos said.

"Why do you care?"

"Bateman and Banks want to replace this whole jungle with bad houses, and they have plans to build a condo here that's so large it'll have its own water park on top of *our* land. They won't quit harassing my father about it. If they get their way, this virgin coast will be a circus." Walking over to the sign, he jerked it up and slid it inbetween the two saddlebags.

"Oh, I didn't know they were harassing y'all. You're *pulling it up*?" she said with a slight smirk.

"We pull them all up, for our collection. They replace them quickly, but we're gonna keep doing it until they stop bothering us."

"But they have a right to buy and sell this land, you know."

"Sure, but the way they do it is wrong. Their houses are overpriced crap, and they butcher the land to build them. Dad is a free market guy, so he'd be okay with it otherwise," he said, and paused. "Now, when people come here to the beach, it's like a nature preserve, you know?"

"I see what you mean. It does feel special here, like how Florida might have been when the Native Americans were roaming around. When I am in the glades, I get that same feeling. It's kind of romantic."

"That's exactly what I am saying. Did you know fireflies still light up here at night?"

"*Yes! I love them.*"

"You know how you can see every star in the sky on a cloudless night from the beach here?"

"Yeah, well, you can't beat that," she said.

"Well, that will all change if they put big, bright condos here," he said, waving his arms at all the surrounding vegetation.

"Yeah, it's pretty sweet being able to see the stars. Did you know you can find your location from any point in the world by them?"

"Celestial navigation? Of course; it's how captains took fleets around the world before GPS."

"That's right," she confirmed.

"You're cool, Leslie. Most girls our age don't know much about this kind of stuff." His intrigue and attraction grew.

"Thanks, Cos—most guys don't know about it either," she said and blushed a little, kicking the heel of her Chuck Taylor on the ground. Cos looked at Dog.

"Dog, get to it." Dog jumped out and crossed the street, lifted his leg on the first For Sale sign and sprinkled it, then he watered the next one, and so on, going down the line.

"Goooood boy," Cos praised. Meanwhile, a black Cadillac Escalade with tinted windows slowly came to a stop behind them.

"Hey, stop that mutt!" a man with matte black Ray-Ban

sunglasses yelled out the driver's window. "Those are our signs!"

Cos pushed the surfboard in front of the sign on the back of his bike and saw Stern Banks.

"Are you the little runt that's been jerking up our signs?" Stern asked Cos through the open passenger window.

"No, sir."

"You're lying to me, boy. Are you that wharf rat's son? Tell him, if he doesn't sell soon, he's going to get what's coming to him. And I am going to have that dog shot the next time I see him whizzing on my signs!"

"Dog? You couldn't catch him if you tried, mister."

"Watch me, boy." Stern stared at Cos for a whole minute to convey something he could never say out loud. Then, he peeled off, revealing his personalized license plate: SOLD.

"Wow, what a jerk," Leslie said.

"Now do you see what we're dealing with?"

"Yeah, but you *were* pulling up their signs."

"Still, it's incredible."

"I know."

They started to pedal again.

"So, are you going to the beach graduation party?" he asked.

"If my parents don't have any plans for me."

"Great, we'll hang out."

"I'd like that," she said, looking down and back up at him, smiling; he grinned and they pedaled on, riding closer now. After about 150 yards, they whipped down Windswept, following it a short way before arriving at Isabella.

From the road, Isabella concealed herself behind a twenty-foot bamboo hedge, save for a slight view through an iron gate, which was frequently left wide open for the Pearl-makers. They entered and cruised down the property's ground oyster shell road; palm trees dotted the driveway in a tightly cut green lawn. At the auto court of the house, the road circled around a hexagonal fountain.

Isabella was a sprawling Italian Mediterranean villa; the exterior wall was constructed of white stucco; terra cotta colored ceramic clay tiles cascaded down the roof. Palm trees, bananas, sago palms, and flowers grew all along the grounds. Plump fruit weighed down branches of various trees and brilliant red roses bloomed underneath the downstairs windows, the smell touching one's nose in the driveway.

"This place is unbelievable, Cosmo!" Leslie gasped, almost dropping her bike.

"Thanks—we make it work."

Hearing a noise, Dog darted off into the distance to patrol the land for varmints, which he practically lived off. He despised being indoors, leaving it for the weaker human species. Unless there was a storm, he stayed in his wooden doghouse by the barn, where he could chase the rats and snakes around the hay. Teddy fed him dog food, but he didn't eat it *really*—instead, he sometimes flipped the bowl over with his paw, scattering the dried pebbles on the ground; then, he tucked away into the shadows of his cave, waiting with patient eyes until a rodent crept up to nibble—then he attacked.

Leslie turned around and saw the barn and Dog's doghouse across from Isabella. On the other side of it sat a workshop. In front of them stood an ancient oak tree, squat and wide and host to an elaborate tree house that had two levels and a swinging bridge connecting the loft-like structures atop it. Electric current ran to it through cables, while big screened windows offered ventilation. Part of an old ship stuck off the first level to the side facing the entrance to the property and the words *Uncle Benny* had been painted across the bottom in black cursive with gold highlights.

"I love the tree house!" she exclaimed, pointing to it.

"That's my big brother Joey's place."

"Your dad built it for him?"

"No, Jojo did most of the work himself, while he was in high school. He always wanted to live in a tree. He's kind of a monkey."

"That's great that your dad let him. I mean, my parents wouldn't."

"Yeah, Dad has always encouraged us to follow our dreams. I want you to meet him. Let's go in and show him the gun."

"Okay."

They leaned the bikes up against the exterior and Cosby removed the pistol and the *Lot for Sale* sign. They entered through the tall mahogany door. At the bottom was a doggy door carved into the dense wood for Dog and their Manx cat, Bear.

"Home sweet home!" he said as they walked down the entrance hall. Fifteen-foot ceilings stretched into the air; bulky brown Spanish clay tiles spanned the floors down the hall into the living room, where they transitioned into thick mahogany planks. Antique paintings hung on white plastered walls, and mahogany timber beams crisscrossed the plastered ceilings.

"This house is *so* beautiful!"

"Thank you. It's old, but Dad has kept it up," Cosby said, looking around with Leslie's fresh eyes. "It requires a lot of maintenance, *and* Joey and I end up doing most of the work."

"That's nice of y'all."

Cos turned to her smiling, "It's *not* optional—he makes

us. Since he inherited the house, he can't afford to pay people to fix it, so it's one of our duties. It's child labor, really. I should have him taken in. Do you want something to drink?"

"Sure."

"Follow me." Going down the hall, they walked through the living room and exited to the right into the dining room, which had windows that overlooked the indoor swimming pool and back porch. Cos called for Teddy, but got no reply. He continued into the kitchen.

Leslie leaned her elbow on the ten-foot-long oak island and applied Chapstick to her lips, while Cos poured them iced glasses of freshly squeezed lemonade. Cos noticed a note scribbled by Charlotte, their maid, stating she had gone out to the grocery store to get supplies for the night's dinner. The two drank the cold lemonade.

"This house is extraordinary, Cos! I just can't get over it."

"Thanks, glad you like it. Let's go see what Teddy thinks about the gun. He's probably out back in the Dog House."

She straightened. "Okay—wait—did you say he's in the Dog House?"

"Well, it's not really a doghouse. You'll see."

They exited through the side kitchen door onto the stone porch and made toward the barn, passing the chicken coop.

"Look at those cute chickens."

"Rhode Island Reds, they're the best chickens. We let them free range. You should come over for breakfast sometime and I'll cook you an omelete. I can cook the perfect omelete."

"That would be nice," she said as they made eye contact.

"Is that a yes?"

"I'll think about it," she said, teasing him a bit.

"*All right*, playing hard to get already and we're not even dating. Just friends."

"Only friends?" she asked, hiding her concern.

"Yeah, I am just looking for a running buddy now. It's *so* nice to have a girl I can just talk to with the pressure off," he said with a straight face. She looked confused.

"I am joking, I am joking. Come on, girl." They came to the workshop and Cos knocked on the wall to the side of the screen door. A crooked wooden sign hung above the door with the words *The Dog House* burned into it; Dog came over from the yard with a bright green lizard tail hanging out of his mouth.

"Come on in!" Teddy boomed from inside.

With Cos holding the screen door for Leslie, she entered and Dog wiggled in after.

"Cos!" Teddy exclaimed with a big grin; he sat on a stool, looking up over his reading glasses, holding a plain ring in his fingers. A steering wheel from an abandoned ship leaned in the corner of the shop, an old bronze diver's helmet rested on the table, and a rack mounted on the ceiling held at least twenty different fishing poles as well as raw wood, spare ceramic tiles, and scrap wood. Tools hung from the pegboard all across one wall, along with two spearfishing bows. In the corner, a gold cage dangled from the ceiling with a blue macaw skirting back and forth. The smell of sandalwood and sawdust hung in the air.

Teddy's skin had the color and texture of worn suede, but without the lines. He rose to greet them.

"Hi Dad, this is Leslie."

"Hi Leslie, it's very nice to meet you. I would shake your hand, but..." He held up his calloused palm, showing her the polishing wax; she noticed he had so many intersecting lines, twice the average person, that he could make a palm reader dizzy.

"That's all right. It's a pleasure to meet you as well," Leslie added. Teddy paid no attention to her lack of an arm.

"It's not too often we have a nice girl around here."

"Oh r-e-a-l-l-y," she said, turning to Cos and smiling.

"No, the only thing Cos ever brings home is that damn dog, and he's usually wet and full of fleas. Not very pleasing on the eyes, either."

"No girls *ever*?"

"*Never*. One day, he trapped a female raccoon outside, but that's about as close as he's ever gotten to love." Teddy gave a wide grin, winking at her.

"Go on you two, drink it up, drink it up. I've dated, I just didn't bring them home because I was too embarrassed by someone's perpetual *shirtlessness*," Cos stressed.

"It's not me, it's you. It's not me, it's you." Teddy paused, smiling. "Well Leslie, you're welcome here at Isabella anytime."

"Thank you! I am enjoying seeing everything. I really love the house. How many rooms are there?"

"Isabella has that effect on most people. She has twenty rooms ... twenty or twenty-one ... I lose count. It's not just her size that gets to you, it's her soul. She's like, *alive!*"

"I think I felt that."

"Well, you're not alone."

"Can I ask why y'all call this the Dog House?" Leslie asked.

"You see, many years ago, when my beloved wife Sarah, God rest her soul, would get mad at me, I would come out here to be quiet and her friends said I was like a bad dog going to the doghouse, and well, I guess the name stuck."

"That's great," Leslie said, pleased by the explanation.

"So what are y'all getting into today?"

"Not much. I got this for you." Cos handed Teddy the for sale sign. Teddy grinned and took it.

"Thanks son, another one for the boneyard." He walked over and speared it into the hanging rack with about twenty others before turning back to them.

"Plus, you're not going to believe what I found while surfing today." Cos took the bandana-wrapped gun and unfolded it on the worktable.

Teddy put on his tortoise readers. "You found this in the surf?

"Yep."

"Oh my—very impressive, son." Focusing on the gun, he plopped back down on the stool and swung over the large magnifying lamp.

"Is it from *La Gracia*?" Cos asked.

"Probably. We'll clean the crust off, then work on dating it. Where did you find it?"

"South of the bay where the best wave breaks are. Near the lighthouse."

"Really?!" He paused, spinning it around in his hands. "The storm must have blown it in. That's about three miles south of where I've been hunting."

"Storms can move ships?" Leslie asked.

"Oh yes my dear, storms have blown in all sorts of treasures. They can carry them for miles." He paused. "You have no idea how much this means to me, son." He smiled and glanced up at Cos over his glasses and then looked back down, studying the pistol for another moment. "I'll start searching in that area right away. I knew today was going to be special. The wind told me. I keep waiting for those damn seagulls to return with another clue, but they never do. They hate me."

"Cos tells me you're looking for a ship that sunk, Mr. Dollarhide?"

"Call me Teddy or Old Salt or Salt or *anything* other than mister."

"Okay, Teddy."

"Thank you. Sportfishing is my main job, but in my spare time, I search for *La Gracia*, a Spanish galleon that went down in the late seventeenth century."

"Interesting! Everyone in my family sails. I would love to hear the story."

"*La Gracia*," Teddy exclaimed with a faraway look in his eyes, wandering into his dreams for a moment. "Admiral García Díaz was in charge of her. She was the pride of a wealthy Spanish prince who commissioned his shipmaster to build him the most impressive galleon to ever sail, but from the beginning, things went terribly wrong with construction. The weather was blazing hot and the men were in agony. A supply wagon carrying the sails from a nearby tailor got robbed and burned. Halfway through construction, lightning struck the deck, setting it on fire, and they had to start all over."

"Good Lord, Dad, you never told me all of that!"

"That's not all! Workers died, too. One fell to his death while erecting the mast; a cannon tipped over on another, crushing his skull. Everyone felt the bad vibe and the shipmaster begged the prince to stop, but he refused. Stubborn bastard. It took years of backbreaking work by hundreds of skilled craftsmen, but they finally produced a ship that took people's breath away. And she sailed off from the port of Seville to a crowd of roaring cheers on her christening. She had collected riches from South America and Cuba and was on her way to North America to gather more gold when she got caught in a brutal hurricane. Out of the vast number on board, only a few made it to shore. The ship carried over twenty-five hundred pounds of gold and an undisclosed amount of silver."

"Whoa!" Leslie said in amazement, stuck to Teddy's every word.

"And there's even more. Gold was the most common smuggled metal, so probably eight times that amount was actually on board. Her metal alone would bring hundreds of millions by today's standards."

"Wowzers!" Leslie exclaimed.

"And that's just the metal. The ship had jewels too," Cos added, nudging Leslie.

"Yes sir. It's rumored there were chests full of emeralds and pearls, and trunks containing valuable antiques."

"It's a gold cove master ship," remarked Cos. "One of the largest and least known treasures ever lost at sea."

"No one has ever found any of it?" Leslie asked, her eyes wide with the thought of riches.

"Only us," Teddy emphasized. "Even historians doubt whether our small finds came from *La Gracia*; many people believe it's a smoke ship—a legend. We have only been able to get small funding for it. No one will really back us, so we're using less than optimal equipment for it. Mainly the magnetometers and sonar and a used ROV I bought online."

"What will you do with the money when you find it?"

"Buy a house in the French Antilles, pay someone to manage this place, and put a lot into charities."

"Don't forget the Sierra Club. We do great work! I work there in the summer. Down in the Everglades."

"I'll remember it. Now, we haven't found it yet," he said, smiling at her.

"Hopefully you'll find it soon," Leslie said.

"Hopefully." He smiled and leaned back on the stool. "So, are y'all getting ready for graduation tomorrow?"

"Yep! Can't wait," Leslie said.

"Good."

"Hey Dad, I passed my final!" Cos said.

"Congratulations, son!"

"Thanks, Dad!"

The royal blue macaw in the corner sang pieces of a Jimmy Buffett song. Dog ran over to the cage, wagging his tail and barking at it.

"That talking bird is funny," she said. Cos walked over to the cage with her.

"That's old Blue," Teddy explained. "He's old now, still sharp as a tack though. Been with me through everything. Got him in Panama when I was there before college. Because of his age, he's sort of a jukebox."

"Dog, get down, leave Blue alone," Cos said.

"Fruitcake," the bird chirped again, laughing at Dog, Cos, and Leslie. Teddy turned around with a smile.

"He hates Dog and Dog hates him. Dog would eat him if he had the chance," Teddy said.

"Fruitcake," the bird chirped.

Leslie laughed.

"Oh Dad, I almost forgot." Cos took out the WANTED poster and unfolded in front of him. Teddy and Leslie both read it. "I thought you'd get a kick out of this."

"*Twenty-five thousand?!* Will Burns must really want that hog dead."

"He was first spotted near the Willis Plantation, so everyone thinks he's possessed or something," Leslie said.

"Oh, that's a bunch of crap," Teddy said.

"Yeah, I know what you mean," Leslie said.

"I am thinking about going over to the Willis Plantation to hunt him for the reward," Cos exclaimed.

"No, son." Teddy's face became serious. "Don't ever go to that place. It's got bad juju."

"But you just said..."

"I know what I said, but I was talking about the hog, not the plantation. That place has been haunted ever since the butterflies left."

"With ghosts?"

"I don't know." He paused. "You know, everything in this town was different before the butterflies left."

"I saw one today," Cos exclaimed.

"What?" Teddy's head jerked up.

"A butterfly."

"That's impossible. It must have been a moth," Teddy insisted.

"No, I am *pretty sure* it was a butterfly."

"It *was* a moth. There are no butterflies here and there never will be any, there aren't even caterpillars wanting to be butterflies—not even the stinging kind. Just stay away from the plantation, okay?" Teddy exclaimed.

"Okay, okay, lighten up, Dad; I won't go to the plantation ... but I do think I saw a butterfly."

Teddy glared at him for a moment. "When does Jojo get here tomorrow?"

"10 a.m."

"Good; I probably won't see him until later in the afternoon because I'll be busy," Teddy said.

Leslie looked at her watch.

"I've gotta get home. Tonight's my sister's sixteenth birthday, and we're having a backyard cookout. I have to help set up. It was so fun hearing about the treasure and your job!"

"Certainly Leslie. It was a pleasure meeting you."

"You too," Leslie said.

"I'll let you know about the gun," Teddy said to Cos as he followed her out.

"Thanks, Dad."

Outside, Cos asked, "So are you coming to the baseball game tomorrow night? It's our qualifier for the regionals."

"I'll be there!"

"Great!"

"I had fun today," she said.

"Me too," he said, and watched her peddle off down the driveway.

~

THE NEXT DAY, Teddy had insisted he would meet Joey at Cosby's graduation. He was very tired for some reason and needed to rest, so he decided to take a nap on the Dog House's sofa with his cat Bear perched on his stomach.

Ram worked the bailing line of the ship. Fatigue shot through his muscles and joints, and his waterlogged shirt weighed down his arms, making it hard to lift the pail. The saltwater clouded and stung his eyes. Strong waves and winds frequently sent him and the bailers sliding back and forth across the floor like marionettes. An officer stepped down through the hatch into the humid galley and yelled to the line for a progress report. The foreman, a bearded muscle-bound man named José, answered in a booming voice, "It rises faster than we can bail, but we're doing our best!"

"Keep working!" he barked over the noise outside. "It'll let up soon!" He exited.

Instructed to retrieve the box for Admiral Díaz, who was now on the deck fighting the violent hurricane, Ram noticed Oscar, the Admiral's pet monkey, enter the room and begin rummaging around the chests, the chest key tight in his black paw. Ram watched him make his way among the sweaty bailing crew. Eventually, he came to the Admiral's chest—a tall square one decorated with a myriad of colors. He stuck the big key in the lock, turned it, and opened the lid, the way he had been trained to do a thousand times before that moment. As he sifted through the contents, he picked up each object, examined it for a moment, and concluding it wasn't the box, threw it over his shoulder; clothes, an ornate silver handheld mirror, and necklaces all went flying. Seeing some jewels packed tightly in gold urns and vases, he picked up a sapphire, bit it, and then tossed it at Ram's back. Ram turned and glared at Oscar, who showed his big teeth. Furious, Ram stomped over and pushed him off the chest. Oscar cowered in the corner and waited for him to leave, then he skirted back over to the chest and found the illustrious box near the bottom. Tucking it under his arm, he made for the hatch. As he neared the opening, a mammoth wave threw the ship to the side. He went flying back; Ram and the crew fell, too, as water rushed in.

The vessel lay sideways. The hatch to the upper deck began to draw water into the body of the ship. Chests filled with gold and jewels toppled and broke open, spilling into the rising water; pearls skated across the floor; a cannon burst out of a wooden box and rolled onto Ram's leg, pinning him down. He grabbed it in pain and opened his mouth to scream, but he didn't have the breath. Rising, the conscious crewmembers waded to the hatch, not knowing Ram was trapped in the corner.

After Ram regained some strength, he yelled out for help, but everyone had already climbed out and above to the side of the ship, which was now a makeshift deck. The saltwater crept up to his chest as he continued to cry out. After ten minutes of calling and struggling to free his throbbing leg, he relaxed with the water at his chin. Tilting his head back, he gained some inches on it. On the floor next to him, he noticed some gold coins and pearls, which he stuffed into his pant pockets. When they were full, he tore off his sleeve, made a pouch of it, and, after loading it with ten pounds of coin, tied a knot in the other end and tucked it in his waistline.

On the other side of the room, Oscar lay on a box, dizzy; he shook his wet head and rubbed the sore part that hit the wall. With the Admiral's box still tucked loosely under his other arm, he rose and climbed from one partially submerged box to another toward the hatch. As he neared it, Ram cried out in the corner. Oscar halted, saw Ram, and climbed over to him, stopping on a box. Seeing the wedged cannon, he waited. He leaned down and reached his arm deep into the water, grabbing some gold coin, which he stuffed into the front pocket of his wet white monkey shirt.

"What are you going to do with that?" Ram remarked under his breath, but Oscar just showed his teeth.

Ram saw a slim scraggly crewmember lowering in to steal some treasure before the ship went down. He made his way over to a wooden chest, busted into it, and filled a rice bag with emeralds, rubies, and what must have been ten pounds of gold. Seeing him, Oscar squealed; when the man made eye contact, the monkey ushered him over with his black paw, jerking his head toward Ram. The man waded over.

"Ram? Is that you?"

"Y-e-ss."

Seeing the cannon and the water below his lips, he tried to move the artillery while Oscar watched.

"It's too heavy, I'll go for help." He waded to the hatch and climbed out. Oscar waited with Ram. A moment later, the man returned with José and another man; the three of them together were able to hoist the cannon off Ram's leg. With the monkey leading, they helped him through the hatch. In the food storage room, the monkey came upon a blue bottle of wine floating in the water next to a few jars of olive oil, and stopped. The men became *frustrated and ushered the monkey on, but he paused and insisted, mesmerized by the wine. He had once snagged a glass of wine that a sailor had left unattended by climbing through an opened cabin window. He remembered how good he felt that day, sunbathing in the crow's nest with heavy eyes. The men pressed on, while the monkey tended to the wine.*

On the makeshift deck, Ram and the men passed the crew who had been dismantling pieces of the destroyed ship to use as rafts. They stopped near Díaz to watch the four rescue boats being loaded amid the pounding rain.

Díaz noticed Ram's hurt leg and assigned him a seat in a boat. "You, next."

"No, I won't go before the others who were here before me."

"What are you, stupid? You'll die floating out there with that leg! Take it!" he said, looking at him with a stern eye. Ram agreed and thanked him. He noticed the regal seal on the pocket of the jacket: a circle with a cross marked through it and a lion's head above the top of it. Diaz spun the knob on his pocket watch clockwise, but not to wind it.

"Why did you do that?" Ram asked.

"I spin it for luck!" he barked. "Wait a minute. There's something important I want you to take to shore." Ram nodded his assent. In a moment, Oscar came around to Díaz's side.

"Where's the box?" Díaz asked. Oscar shook his head in the negative and pointed down below.

Díaz grunted, almost laughing, "Have you been drinking again?"

The monkey held his fingers up indicating a pinch. "Never send a monkey to do a man's job. Well, there's nothing we can do about it now." Oscar climbed up Díaz's wet jacket sleeve to his broad shoulder, where he sat. Then, Díaz waved Ram off to two men who helped lower him into one of the overstuffed boats. The oarsmen pushed away toward the invisible coastline, belting

"Good luck" to the men on the ship. *The nose of the little boat pointed to the sky and dipped back down as it floated over mammoth swells. Ram looked up at the furious sky, watching it roar and rage. Sadness overtook him as he felt there was something he was leaving behind—something very important, and it wasn't Díaz's box. He couldn't remember what it was, so he closed his eyes. The world went black.*

Teddy jerked up on the sofa, his eyes big and round. The sound of the storm reverberated in his mind like an annoying vacuum. He looked around his room for the wet men or the monkey, but everything was dry and empty. Grabbing his aching leg, he glanced down and saw the birthmark in the same place that the cannon had landed. He shook his head, glanced at his watch, and, realizing Cosby's graduation was thirty minutes away and that he had slept through the morning—he jumped up, ran his hand through his hair, stroked his beard and headed out the door.

3

J oey Dollarhide forgot how hot Florida got in the summer, and this summer was even hotter than usual, with every day breaking the previous record for that date. He watched his brother Cosby receive his diploma at the graduation service that afternoon with his father, and the after-party was now underway at Lover's Bay Park, with the Florida sun beating down on the assembly like a hot bleeding furnace.

For the past four years, Joey had been at UCLA. In his senior year at Latch High, he was the best hitter in the state, taking the Indians to a regional championship, which earned him a full ride with the UCLA Bruins. His junior year at UCLA, he was supposed to be the next big ball sensation after a YouTube video of a 575-foot bomb he slugged during a UCLA Bruins versus Oregon Ducks game went viral, but he tore his ACL before the last game of the season and it required surgery. And he hadn't torn it sliding into home plate or diving for a line drive—he tore it by accidentally running his bicycle into the Oregon Ducks mascot while waving at a girl across campus. He told the coach it was a surfing accident, but an ecology student was video-taping a group falconry project outside and captured the whole thing in the background. Then, she did him the lovely "favor"—her words—of uploading it to YouTube. Now the "Oregon Duck Hunt" video had more views than his big bomber. Although his leg felt fine now, the doctors said he could never play again without reinjuring it. Goodbye majors, hello forestry. A solid collegiate career with a depressing end, but he felt better now in Latch's arms —like slipping into a broken-in pair of leather shoes.

For young people in Latchawatchee, the aura of summer started with the graduation celebration for the seniors and their families at the postcard park on the water. All the students from Latch High attended; food vendors of all types had booths, white tents with tables were sprawled across the grass lawn. The park was the perfect setting for the event, with its wide oaks and limbs that dripped with hanging silver moss, robust palms, and manicured lawn. Violets, milkweed, and banana plants nestled in beds with a path that snaked alongside them. A Moorish tiled fountain sat in the center of the park surrounded by a rose garden featuring white, red, and yellow blooms.

As Joey navigated the maze of bodies, many dressed in black graduation gowns, acquaintances gave him an elbow pound and old friends hugged him. Some young ladies tucked their hair behind their ears and tailed him, asking if he was going to the beach party tomorrow. He told them yes with a smile, but in the back of his mind he was concerned that *she* would be there.

Annabelle "Belle" Burns had transferred to Latch her senior year from College Station, Texas. Her father was a Texas high school dropout who rolled the dice wildcatting with his savings when he was twenty-two and struck the black gold lotto. With over one hundred million in the bank twenty-five years later, he decided to move the family to Florida to semi-retire, take a stab at real estate, and manage his wells from a distance. A young but lucrative and growing real estate company based out of Jacksonville, Bateman and Banks, had contacted him in search of an angel investor. After agreeing to meet them, they picked him up at dusk on a seventy-foot Sunseeker yacht at the marina, got him drunk on Ketel One and caviar, and made a proposal. Dazzled by their big returns, Ivy-League connections, and Zegna shoes, the cowboy from Texas was sold. Maybe he felt that being connected to them somehow validated him, for with all the millions, a new last name was the one thing he hadn't been able to buy—and he wanted to be *old* money. When he wasn't on the phone, he spent his days golfing in Latch or yachting to the Bahamas. His daughters, Belle, Paige, and Courtney, lived a life of four-course meals and designer ensembles.

From the moment Joey first saw Belle swishing down the hall their senior year of high school, she struck him like lightning cracking a tree. She was a master at make-believe, and he, a seasoned dreamer. The world was her stage, and the people around her were characters in the story of her life; everyone else was a faithful audience along for the adventure. Her story was about the sea, and her blue eyes were a door to the ocean. On the stage of her imagination, anything was possible—even the mundane laws of nature didn't apply to her. Her auburn hair was like a prop, hanging down to her butt and whipping like a horse's tail as she walked. Some days it seemed a lot shorter, too—when she wanted it to be. She was five foot eight, had a big cartoonish mouth, and ears that stuck out to the sides. Joey liked how angelic she looked, but it was her creative mind that crushed him.

He'd wasted no time asking her out, but Zach Watts beat him to it. To Joey's bewilderment, they stayed together all throughout senior year, breaking up just before graduation. The next week, a friend invited Joey and Cos on a Catalina cruise at sunset and Belle came along with her friend Natasha. Joey slipped into the deep end every time he looked in Belle's aqua eyes. When the boat took a quick turn, she fell into him, spilling her drink on his shirt; he braced her fall by taking her hand, and they laughed at the touch. On the way back to the harbor, she got a chill from the wind and he let her borrow his windbreaker. She was leaving the next week for an internship in Paris, and he was going to the Bruins' training camp in Los Angeles. He called her and they quickly became friends. One day, she mentioned a Parisian she was dating, and Joey kicked over a trashcan and started dating his new best friend in Malibu, the sponsored surfer Adrianna. Adrianna was athletic, sweet, Greek, spoke four languages, and he loved her, but when he looked into her brown eyes, he wasn't in the deep end. There were things about life that he couldn't talk to her about—things he sensed Belle would understand. When he went home for breaks, he saw Belle here and there, and magic always seemed to follow them. In the spring, she Facetimed him the day after she broke up with the Parisian whom she had dated long-distance for a while after returning to the University of Texas, but Joey was still with Adrianna. Her heart dropped and she sighed, but she had trouble seeing past the long distance anyway. Joey broke up with Adrianna a couple of months later; but by the time he Facetimed Belle, she was dating someone new. Fate had been a terrible foe once again.

She was like the ocean coming to him with the tide, and he was the sand. When they connected, she would soften his rough exterior and when she rolled away, she would take a little mica with her, holding the pieces of him until they were lost in the vastness of her. And he would cling to her saltwater until it evaporated off his surface, and then, empty and longing, they would need each other again. And so the tide rolled in and out, and the sand waited patiently for the day when the ocean would rise and they could be one.

The chemistry peaked last July at a mutual friend's wedding in Montana where they made each other laugh so hard they began to cry, falling on the floor, unable to catch their breath. When they looked up at each other red-eyed and sore faced, they were both in the deep end and wanting to go deeper. He petted her hair and she closed those aqua eyes and slinked her arms around his strong shoulders, but when his lips got close, she pulled away, stood up, and ran out the door into the rain, crying, because she was still taken and he lived too far away. He followed after her, but she jumped into her car and retreated into the sea again. And her play went on, and Joey realized hers was a love story and he was the male lead. Only this time, when the memory of her left him, he wouldn't wait. He had his own story to live; the dramatic short scenes where their stories overlapped couldn't sustain him.

So senior year he dated, did some light surfing his leg could sustain on the weekends, and studied hard. He and Belle didn't talk or write, and by spring, he had learned to forget about her. When he booked his ticket home for Cosmo's graduation and a friend told him Annabelle Burns was single again, he shrugged it off with as much care as if they had told him it was going to rain.

Wiggling through the crowd of familiar faces with a big

grin, he finally spotted Cos with Dog, talking to some friends.

"Cosmo!" Joey shouted.

Cos turned and saw him. "Jojo!" Opening their arms, they walked toward each other.

"Congratulations! Damn it's good to see you!" Joey said as they hugged, smiling.

"Thanks! You too. Man, I've *really* missed you."

"I've missed you too. It's a nice day to graduate."

"It sure is, but it's hot. Every day breaks a new record."

"That's what I hear. I love it though. I miss a 90-degree day."

"So you're finally done with UCLA?"

"Yep, it's been great, but I've taken a lot of shit about the duck video. Someone even made T-shirts."

"Tees? Ouch, I am sorry to hear it."

"Yeah, but I've got tough skin. Lately, I've really missed Isabella, you, and Dog."

"And Teddy?"

"*And even Dad.* We stood next to each other during the ceremony, but he had to meet The Pearlmakers at the marina afterwards and we didn't get to catch up, really. He told me he'd catch us back at the house."

"Yeah, the old man missed the sea too much. Actually, I found a pistol while surfing the other day and showed it to him. He thinks it may be from *La Gracia.*"

"*Really?* Was it one of those old long-nosed pistols?"

"Yes sir, gold finished too."

"Where'd you find it?"

"South of the bay near the lighthouse. He's going to start searching there today."

"Sweet."

Joey reached down and picked up Dog by the stomach,

holding him against his V-neck T-shirt; his tongue hung out as he craned his head back.

"Hey little buddy, it's been a long time."

"Dog and I caught some good waves today from the storm two days ago. It's still a third the size of a Mavericks wave, but big for Florida. Did you hear about Hurricane Eliza?"

"Just a little on the news in the Houston airport."

"She started out as a small tropical, but she's all grown up now. Supposed to make landfall early morning the day after tomorrow."

"Ouch, that's bad."

"I know. But, it sounds like the annual beach bash tomorrow night is still on."

"Yeah, all of the alumni are going to be there. You want to break open some cold ones?"

"Of course. What's going on tonight?" Cos said.

"I just want to eat oysters with the old man and go swimming."

"Sounds good to me. Walk with me. I got to find Wolly."

"Sure, how is big Wolly?"

"The same, but bigger. He can barely round the bases now," Cos said, and Joey laughed.

Walking through the crowd, they passed various tents set up in the park. Dog trotted by Cos's side on a tight leash. Wooden booths showcased fresh pies and delicacies baked by competitive old women displaying their skills.

They passed the center of the park where a crowd gathered, gazing in a concerned manner at the fountain, which bubbled with white foam overflowing onto the concrete around it. The smell of laundry detergent burned their nostrils; Dog sneezed. Two police officers with flat tops drilled a lanky thirteen-year-old wearing an Affliction shirt and baggy jeans about the incident. Cos and Joey grinned as they walked by.

"Someone pulled another bubble bath prank with laundry detergent in the fountain," Cos said.

"Not as original as the cow—I heard about that one."

"I can't believe the boys did that, the teachers are pissed about it," Cos whispered, looking around. "I drove them out to campus, but they said they didn't know what they were going to do. I had no idea. Shhhhh. Don't tell anyone I was there." He looked around to the sides.

"You were there. Ha! Don't worry about it." He gestured with his hands. "If you didn't know and didn't help, you're clear."

They kept walking and passed a Disneyland-style line in front of Dan's World Famous Fried Chicken booth. Dan, a short man from Breaux Bridge, Louisiana, with a bald head that reflected light, took orders, counting them with his fingers in the air in a thick Cajun accent. His stomach was a portable advertisement for the irresistibility of his chicken and biscuits, for "that boy has tore up some biscuits," as Teddy liked to point out. Despite the restaurant's fast food décor of lipstick red booths and highlighter yellow walls, people came from all over the Southeast to try his fried chicken. A swank New York chef once got wind of it, offering Dan fifty thousand dollars for the recipe. Dan said the figure was embarrassing and called the man a "thieving yellow-bellied scoundrel" before challenging him to "just bring it on down to Florida for a fistful of manners." In fact, practically the only time Dan wasn't irate was when he was singing Broadway show tunes around the kitchen.

Cos had worked the fryer and driven the delivery truck for Dan since the tenth grade. He disliked it with a passion, but it was easy money and he was given free access to the car. As long as he made his deliveries, he could use the car for some personal things.

Cos ducked behind the crowd to avoid Dan's eye, and Joey followed. They spotted Wolly talking to Paige, Belle's younger sister, standing under a tree beside the One Hundred Egg Cake stand. She twiddled her brunette hair with one hand and laughed at everything Wolly said, touching his arm with the other hand—her biggest competition was his plate of chicken.

Joey and Cos approached as Belle glided over from the side with a plate of cake, the ground glowing beneath her step. The sight of her split an atom in Joey's sleeping heart. In one year, Annabelle Burns had passed through that mysterious realm from immature girl to confident young woman, and her new presence leveled Joey—his face went numb and his mouth felt like he had been chewing on gum for hours.

Belle tilted her head slightly forward and grinned at Paige and Wolly while she listened and ate her cake. She laughed with them, showing her big teeth. A white bandage covered her left eye from cheek to forehead; when she saw Joey and Cos approaching out of her other eye, she brushed her sun-washed red hair across her face, tucked it behind her ear, and smiled at them before looking back at Wolly and Paige. She had a radiant glow that brought a cold sweat to Joey's palms.

"Boone!" Cos yelled.

Wolly swallowed a big mouthful of chicken and answered. "Well, look here, it's the Dollarhides! My favorite family. What's happening?" he said.

"Not much, I just came in from California," Joey replied.

"Well, it's great to see you again, bud." Wolly threw his arm around Joey and hugged him close to his black graduation gown, which had the smell of John Varvatos. His hair was clean-cut.

"Wolly, you know coach told you to lay off that stuff," Cos added.

"What coach doesn't know won't hurt him."

"Congratulations on the game last night!" Joey said.

"Thanks, but I couldn't have done it without your brother. He drove in the winning run."

"Thanks, Boone. The pitcher had a weak fastball." Cos paused. "Has anyone seen Leslie?"

"She had to go home early; her aunt and uncle are in town," Paige said.

"That's a bummer," Cos said.

"You got it bad for that girl—Leslie, Leslie, Leslie, that's all I ever hear about," Wolly said.

"Shut up, Boone," Cos said. "We're just friends."

"Yeah, *okay*," remarked Wolly.

"Congratulations on graduating!" Cos said to Paige.

"Thanks, Cos! I am so glad it's over."

"Ready to be a Miami Hurricane?" Cos asked.

"Yep, dad offered to pay my way and get me a little house in Coconut Grove."

"Sweet!" Joey said.

"Hey guys, do you remember my sister Belle?" Paige asked.

"Of course," Joey said, making eye contact. "How've you been? I haven't seen you since last summer."

"Really great! How 'bout you?"

"That's great! I am doing good," Joey said. "That cake looks outstanding."

"Did you know they use one hundred eggs to make that cake?" Wolly asked.

"I kind of figured that from the name, Wol," Joey said.

"It's really good! Want a bite?" Belle asked.

"Sure!" She offered Joey the fork and he took a bite; the sugar melted in his mouth and it was even sweeter coming from her.

"Isn't it good?" Belle asked.

"Oh yeah, that's maybe the best cake I've ever had."

"Hey Cos, tell the girls about the senior prank," Wolly said.

"Shut up, Boone! I wasn't even a part of it."

"Who gives a crap!" Wolly said. "We've graduated now. They can't take our diplomas away, this isn't the Heisman you know."

"Come on, tell us ... *please!*" Paige begged.

"I am not telling because I didn't even know what was going on. I just dropped them off in the chicken. I didn't even know what they were doing."

"I'll tell everyone then, y'all just promise not to tell anyone," Wolly said.

"We promise," Paige and Belle said.

"Okay, well, you know Betsy?" Wolly smiled and pointed to himself.

"That was you?" Paige said. He nodded in agreement. "Oh my God."

Belle cracked a laugh and exclaimed, "I saw her when I was visiting campus yesterday. I walked by and she actually mooed."

"She mooed in midair?" Joey asked.

"Midair," Belle said.

"Nice," Joey said.

"It's kind of animal cruelty though," Cos said.

"Is the cow hurt, Cos?" Wolly asked.

"No," answered Cos.

"Did people laugh?" Wolly said.

"I guess."

"Then it's fine. You worry too much," Wolly said.

Wolly finished off his chicken and got in line for cake. Paige and Cos joined him, inviting Joey, but he declined. Belle glanced down at the ground before looking back up at Joey.

"I like the flower in your hair. The white looks good with your blue eyes," Joey said, flirting. She blushed a little and smiled.

"Thanks—my one blue eye now. A lady at one of the booths just gave it to me. She said the Hawaiian Plumeria flower are a flower of charm and grace."

"I need to be wearing one, then."

"Yeah, you should get one." She broke a wide smile.

"Is your eye okay?"

"Yeah, it's just a little bruised. I got hit in the face with a boomerang the other day while walking across campus."

"*A boomerang?* I am sorry to hear that. That's weird!"

"Yeah, things like that happen to me."

"So I've been meaning to call you. Just—got busy, you know?"

"It's okay. I meant to call you, too. I thought about you, though."

"I thought about you too. Still in Austin?"

"Yep, I just finished school. It's been a great four years, but I am looking forward to a change."

"What are you doing next?"

"I want to go to Stanford for my MBA."

"California, really?" His eyes lit up.

"Yeah, I just love it out there. The Mediterranean climate reminds me of our family trips to Greece when I was younger."

"Maybe we can meet up sometime on the West coast."

"I'd really like that. What are you doing next?"

"I've signed up to be a forest ranger in California."

"How fun! Like putting out fires and stuff?"

"Mainly patrolling, population control, and monitoring. Possibly managing some ground fires. I'd love to smoke jump, but they won't let me with my injury."

"I've *always* wanted to smoke jump."

"You know there aren't many girls doing that."

"Yeah, well, there aren't many *girls* doing a lot things I wanna do. It just looks like so much fun."

"I know what you mean."

"Oh baby, this cake is so good!" Wolly said, coming back over with the plate close to his face as he ate. Cos and Paige followed with plates of their own.

"I guess Dan didn't make you work today?" Wolly asked Cos.

"No, he let me off."

Belle leaned down and petted Dog. "You're pretty sweet to be a surfer dog." He tried to lick her face. When he connected, she moved away. "And feisty too."

Paige looked around, then knelt on the ground, examining it.

"What are you looking for?" Belle asked.

"My bracelet is missing. The clasp was loose. It must have fallen off," she said nervously. "I've got to find it. Mom just gave it to me as a graduation present."

"I am sure it's around here somewhere," Belle said, kneeling to look with her. They looked for a few minutes— Paige growing more distressed by the second—Wolly went down to help.

"It was our great grandmother Lulu's; I *have* to find it," Paige remarked.

"Lulu's bracelet?? Oh my God, we *do* have to find it," Belle said.

"Was it gold?" Cos asked.

"Yes," Paige said.

"Good." Cos took off his thin gold necklace and held it to Dog's nose; then he said in a strong voice, "Hunt boy!" Hearing the words, Dog darted forward with his nose to the ground. He stopped here and there to sniff along a zigzagging line, in the general direction that Paige had come from. Finding the bracelet, he picked it up and tracked back to Cos, stopping in front of him where he dropped it, waiting for his reward.

"He found it?!" Paige said, walking toward him. "How did he find it?"

"Good boy! He sniffs gold," Cos said. He picked it up and petted Dog. He poured his water over the bracelet to clean it and handed it to Paige, then he took out a sandwich bag of turkey jerky from his pocket and handed a chunk to Dog, who gobbled it up.

"Thank you *so much!*" Paige said.

"You're welcome!"

"How on earth did he do that?" Belle said.

"Teddy trained him to smell gold after learning about Peter Bergman, CEO of the Swedish company OreDog training Arctic canines to sniff for ore and gold," answered Cos.

Dog sat with his tongue hanging out, staring up at the crowd, basking in the attention.

"That's incredible," Belle said.

"Oh, I was so worried I'd lost it. You're an angel, Dog," said Paige.

Wolly wrapped his arm around her shoulder and she purred at the contact.

"I didn't know Dog could smell gold," Wolly said.

"Yep, that's Dog. I am glad he was here to help," Cos said, looking down at Dog, admiring his little friend. "He looks tired from this heat, though. I'm going to take him home."

"I am with you, Cosby. Can I crash at your house tonight?" Wolly added.

"*Mi casa es tu casa.*"

"It was nice talking with you girls," Joey said with a smile. "See you at the beach tomorrow night?"

"We'll be there," they said.

"Perfect!"

Belle bent her fingers forward and up and down with a smile to Joey. Walking away from her was like prying himself off a king-sized magnet.

"Hey Cos, I am riding with Joey," Wolly said.

"You don't want to ride with me?"

Wolly shook his head in disagreement. Joey put on his tortoiseshell Persols and laughed. They headed over to where Joey had parked his 1961 golden wheat-colored Chevy Impala convertible with California plates on the other side of Route 1 and hopped in. The hot leather steering wheel stuck to Joey's hands. When he cranked the engine, Smokey Robinson blasted out of the stereo; the A/C blew on high, but didn't give much cool air.

Joey glimpsed Cos and Dog in the rearview as they went into the neighborhood across the street to Dan's delivery vehicle. He and Wolly laughed as they watched him get in the 1972 Pontiac Grand Safari station wagon painted bright yellow with red trim. Dan had bolted a three-foot-tall red and yellow chicken head to the roof and a matching tail feather on the back and even installed a personalized rooster horn. Slanted red letters on the side door read "Dan's World Famous Fried Chicken" with a phone number below. Cos took a lot of criticism at school for driving it, but like his nickname, he didn't care much.

He pulled away and Joey peeled out in front of him, catching a breeze. They cruised north on Route 1 past the mansions that lined the bay toward the ocean. Dog stuck his head out the window with his tongue flying. The road hugged the coastline, and Joey felt at home when he saw the Atlantic again. Wolly suggested picking up some beer, so they stopped off at Bert's Gas and Bait Shop to get a twelve-pack of Blue Moon bottles before driving back to the farm.

When they arrived at Isabella, Teddy's brown zebu bull Five Alarm skirted off into the distance. Teddy had a bad habit of leaving the gate to the back thirty acres open, and whenever he did, Five Alarm ran wild. The group went straight for the outside cooler that Teddy kept stocked with wild game and fish from his excursions. Joey took out a handful of ahi tuna steaks, thawed them in warm water, cut them up, sea-salted them, and put them on an oval platter. Then, they went around through the ivy-covered gate into the backyard with the fish and beer. Tropical vegetation covered the area around the pool, giving it the appearance of a rainforest. A large oak tree sat between the left side of the pool and the stucco wall; a rope the boys used to swing into the pool hung from one of the branches closest to the pool's edge. A rattletrap wooden pool house was on the other side of the pool. They sat at the teak tables on the slate porch and, after grilling the fish, ate the plump pink tuna steaks with sea salt and chased it with cold coriander ale. Afterwards, they went swimming with Dog, who frequently jumped out and ran the perimeter of the 500 square foot pool, appearing like an ocean in the blessed night. Fireflies flickered at the edge of the yard near the segos as the boys swam and joked about girls and life.

4

Teddy trolled on an even longitude with the old hunting location, three miles north and four hundred yards east from where Cos found the pistol. The GPS tracker beeped. Each area they had dived and come up empty-handed was marked with a red dot; any point where a piece from *La Gracia* was found was marked with a green dot.

Glancing over at the small Manx sitting on the captain's dash, his mini captain's hat crooked as he monitored the horizon, Teddy smirked.

Bear was a big thing in a small package. His back legs were longer than his front, and he had a kind of strut like a 1950s greaser. Teddy always caught him bothering the female cats twice his size, even when the season was wrong. He could climb a tree, and unlike ordinary cats who just jump out of trees, he could climb back down. And ever since his miraculous recovery from feline AIDS, Bear had a passion for the ocean that no other cat had ever known. Teddy petted him while studying the GPS.

From the dream, Teddy knew the treasure was in the

hull—gold was often stored there for ballast; he also knew there were boxes of cannons in the hull for backup, like the one that rolled on his leg. They were searching for a cannon or a chest of gold, silver, or jewels—any clue as to where the hull might be.

The rest of The Pearlmakers—Patrick, Ty, and Dallas—relaxed in the back of the boat, shooting the breeze. Patrick, or "Patch," was a professor of archaeology and history at the University of Miami who wanted nothing more than to work on an offshore treasure hunt during his summers. He was wearing circular glasses, a tank top, and a Miami Hurricanes baseball cap creased heavily at the bill. A nice intellectual type who added organization to the brash crew, his extensive knowledge of Spanish history had helped Teddy correctly document, trace, and date many of the items in the catalog.

Usually the first to go down, Ty was the best diver in the group. He had curly brown hair and a face that appeared carved out of stone with a constant five o'clock shadow. In the 90s, he was a commercial scuba diver on combat pay for oil rigs in the Gulf. He had a long scar on his right forearm where a barracuda bit into him last year and wouldn't let go; Dallas was the one to spear it just before the beast could chew the arm clean off. After some stitches, Ty was in the water two days later, against his doctor's orders.

Dallas, or "Dal," was a black linebacker and a student of Teddy's at the University of Miami. He was selected in the first round of the NFL draft, but he withdrew at the last minute to study plankton instead. He went onto earn his PhD in marine biology after leaving the university and later worked on the recovery of the *SS Central America*. His strength went a long way with the lifting of heavy items underwater, and he was the whiz of the operation—Dal knew it all, knowledge he gained from his days working on the search for the SS *Central America*.

The sun swirled in the sky, its reflection skipping off the water with the ripples of the waves. The oceanfront houses in Latch dotted the distant shore. Teddy dropped the anchor. Ty and Dal jumped in the blue water, splashing like fallen boulders. They dived to the bottom to explore the midnight maze of the ocean floor.

Teddy sat back in his captain's chair, gazing out toward the endless horizon. His blue eyes squinted in the luminescent sun as he stroked Bear on the back, reflecting about the gun and the six years they had spent searching for *La Gracia*.

While visualizing the massive fortune hiding below, he dreamed about helping others. It was Sarah's dream, really —"No one should die of hunger," she used to say. She worked three months out of the year in the Sudan to bring food to villages in need, putting up with constant bureaucratic BS to thwart her efforts or divert funds, but she always stayed strong and held her position. Even through the cancer, she was optimistic. She had a natural radiance to her that didn't fade when her body did; instead, she seemed to glow even more as her time neared.

After her death, Teddy began to feel that there was some connection between health and the food people consumed. At least in his mind, he believed good nutrition could go a long way toward preventing cancer. He put the whole family on traditional whole foods and vegetable and fruit juices. He cooked a lot, exploring the benefits of certain herbs, foods, and flavors and their synergies.

Teddy swigged his Nalgene bottle of ice water and poured Bear some in a tin cup attached to a Velcro patch below the dash. Bear lapped at it and the act made Teddy smile.

He remembered how Sarah loved to sing. He used to play the piano, and they would sing together for hours. She loved plants and working in the garden with her round-brimmed straw hat, basking in the sun. She was tall with curly red hair and little bitty features. When she worked outside, he would bring her iced tea and she would wipe the sweat from her brow and teach him about each plant: what the species was and where it originated. Plants were her passion, but helping others was her religion; she would give her last piece of food to someone who needed it more.

Patch slid the door open with an ear-splitting grin, informing him that Dal and Ty found something. Bear turned at attention as Teddy rose and headed to the deck. Bear trailed him, hopping on a cooler outside to watch the crew work. Dal propped up on the boat in the water and told Patch to lower the hoister. Ty rose up after him, resting on the landing.

"Jackpot, Teddy. We've got something big!" Dal said. After raising himself up, he sat on the side of the boat with his legs still in the water. The yellow scuba tank looked like a child's backpack on him.

"Is it something good?" Patch asked.

"Is it from the hull?" Teddy pressed.

"It's a cannon, this time with *no base!*" Dal said, smiling.

"Well, if that don't put pepper in the gumbo! Are you thinking what I'm thinking, Dal?"

"It could be from the hull. A boxed cannon for backup."

"Well I'll be damned. This ain't chicken shit boys, it's chicken salad!" Teddy brushed Bear off the cooler and grabbed two ice-cold water bottles, tossing one to Dal and the other to Ty.

"What do you think, Ty?" Teddy asked.

"Well, it could be from anywhere on the ship, but I

reckon it's from the hull because it doesn't have a base," Ty explained.

"Hot dog!" barked Teddy.

"Of course, we couldn't have done it without Cosmo," Dal said, chuckling.

"Yeah, the chip off the old block!" Teddy exclaimed.

"Do you think it could be from another ship?" Patch asked.

"Could be. As you know, there are no other records of ships going down here. That doesn't mean it never happened. The ocean is full of undocumented ghost ships, but I reckon she drifted over the years," Teddy said.

"Do you think it went down here or at the other site?" Dal asked.

"If the hull is here, this is probably where she finally went down, or she drifted!" Teddy barked. "Of course, we'll have to pay off our crew debts with any profits from it, nothing really to keep afterward, but at least we're on the right track. How does it look down there?"

"Pretty clean job, just sitting on the sand. We used the blower and blasted under about two feet of sand. There are a couple of reef sharks down there, though. Pass me the spear gun just in case," Dal said.

Teddy opened a large square chest bolted to the deck behind the captain's house. Removing the spear gun and some arrows, he handed them to Dal.

"The load is quite heavy, Salt. We're going need an extra hand down there to get it in the harness," Ty said.

"Patch, man the boat, I'm going down with them. Throw Dal the steel cables from the crane and feed him slack as he goes down," Teddy said.

"Okay, good luck!" Patch hollered.

Teddy removed his unbuttoned short-sleeved white

linen shirt and threw it to the side. Then, he laid down the Panama hat and slung on a scuba pack. After adjusting to the tank, he kissed the gold St. Nicholas pendant around his neck and jumped into the water. Dal took the cable and jumped in after, Ty following.

They dove deep. Large underwater flashlights illuminated the murky water. When they reached the bottom, Dal pointed to the black rusty lump of coal and Teddy studied it, running his hand along its surface. His eyes smiled as he flipped a thumb up. Teddy and Dal held the arms up, while Ty wrapped the harness around it. They couldn't hold the heavy weight for long. When the harness was tight around it, they tugged on the cables hard, signaling Patch to start the crane. To the side of the box, Dal saw and picked up a blue bottle of the wine they'd dredged up six months ago. Patch started to raise the load slowly; mud dispersed into the water as it lifted from the ocean floor; they swam up with it.

They broke the surface, climbed into the boat, and removed their scuba gear. As the crane lifted it out, Teddy recognized it as one of the baseless cannons in the hull from his dreams. Patch swung it into the boat with the crane, then slowly lowered it to the floor while the men guided it with their hands.

Teddy petted the crusted piece with his arm like a long-lost friend, and they all marveled at the artillery from *La Gracia's* hull. Teddy let out a loud hoot. The crew exchanged hugs, congratulating each other. They had been searching for a clue like this for years. Teddy retrieved some Cohiba Habanos cigars from his swag box in the cabin, and they smoked them, watching the sun drop.

On the way back to the marina, while rummaging through a storage closet on *Gold Lip*, Teddy came across the box containing the twelve blue bottles of wine they'd pulled up from *La Gracia*. He shook his head, thinking about Bear and the feline AIDS a year ago. The veterinarians had sent the cat home with a medical death sentence. Teddy tried everything, but as time passed, Bear grew weaker. When the spark left his eyes and he started moping around the farm with his head down, Teddy became distraught. Sitting in his captain's chair one day over a year ago, Teddy's eyes had fallen upon one of the twelve blue quart-sized bottles. They had agreed to not open them, but thinking it would relax him, Teddy unhinged the wire cap, uncorked it, and poured a short glass of the 300-year-old ferment. The first sip twisted his face. No doubt it was good, but tart. After finishing the glass, he felt full, peaceful, light. The next day, he woke with more energy and vitality—his sinuses were clear for the first time in years. What the hell had happened?

He decided to give some to Bear, starting him on a minute dosage. Bear lapped it up. Within two weeks, some of his energy returned. Within four, he was bothering the female cats again and killing rats in the barn. A month later, the vet gave him a clean bill of health.

Teddy sent a sample of the wine to a lab rat buddy in Cambridge, Massachusetts, who gave it to cancerous mice. Within two weeks, they were cured. News spread like wildfire through the facility, and two weeks later, his friend got a death threat, his credit cards were canceled, and he was laid off. Locked out of the lab, he stopped returning Teddy's calls and disappeared.

So, Teddy recently started having his own tests run on the wine, and so far, he'd had no feedback. He knew it wasn't just the age; rather, it seemed there was an element added to it either accidentally or consciously that created a healing synergy. Whatever it was, Teddy was convinced the Spaniards had unknowingly discovered a sort of elixir.

Coming out of his reverie and closing the door, he walked back over to the captain's chair and watched as the boat chugged toward the marina.

HOURS HAD PASSED at Isabella when the boys heard the sound of two trucks coming down the driveway followed by the familiar screech of the Ford's brakes. A moment later, Teddy entered the backyard carrying two bushels of oysters in one hand and a plastic bucket in the other, the remainder of a Cuban plug stuck in his mouth; Dallas walked behind him. Joey jumped out of the pool, toweled himself off, and ran over to hug his father. Teddy's bare chest was hot to the touch. He greeted his son and asked the whole group if they would like some oysters. They all agreed.

Teddy took off his Panama hat, set it on the teak table, and combed his fingers through his pearl-white hair and stroked his beard generously. Then, he took a seat. He and Dal kidded the boys about swimming under the influence of the beer. Teddy took six oyster knives out of the bucket and set them on the table. He always had enough to go around because the only thing he liked more than eating oysters was sharing them.

The thick wet night grew more alive with the song of the crickets, cicadas, and frogs, and the fireflies now speckled the backyard like blinking lights on a dancing Christmas tree.

The group hovered around the table and began to shell a bushel, using their knives to eat and tossing the empty shells into the white bucket with thuds and clangs. Teddy told them the oysters were Blue Points from up north. They were small, but the briny taste was like swimming in the Atlantic on a sun baked day. They chased the saltiness with the ale as Teddy informed them about the cannon. He thanked Cos again for finding the gun. Then, he asked Joey more about California, and Joey told him while they ate and drank. Joey rubbed Dog's belly with his foot as Dog lay on the stone floor, struggling to hold his eyelids open.

The group finished off the bushel and went to see the cannon as Teddy and Dal unloaded it into the preservation room. They expressed amazement and took a round of photos with it. Joey got a look at the pistol as well before he, Cos, and Wolly retired.

Teddy and Dal hoisted the cannon up with a Bobcat lift and set it down in a box of fresh water designed to dissolve the crustacean. They cataloged the date and time, locked up, and left.

UNDER THE GLOW of the reading lamp in his bedroom, Teddy examined through his reading glasses the ring they'd found last week wound up in tattered clothes buried deep in the sand. He concluded it was a wedding ring: a pitiful thing really, made of ivory and only fit for a peasant, worthless, the bone chipped, but he couldn't stop thinking about its history.

"Every object has a tale to tell," his father, Jim, used to say. As a teenager when he tagged along for his father's hunts after the treasure of the French pirate of the Gulf of Mexico, Jean Lafitte, around Fort Morgan, Alabama where it was rumored the pirate had buried some of his ten million dollar treasure, and they found artifacts, his dad would ask him to tell a tale for each item on the truck ride home. The game was fun, and sometimes his stories matched up pretty close to the truth when they eventually discovered where and when the item was born, who it belonged to, and what it was made out of. But Jim would always conclude by looking at him with wizened eyes and saying that "only God knows *everything* an object has seen: the love, victories, defeats, conceptions, transformations."

Where are the chests of gold? Who did you belong to? Tell me your secrets, poor ring—let me see with your ivory eyes, so I can know what you know.

He turned off the light, removed his readers, and closed his heavy eyes. What a poor ring, he thought again with it clutched in the fault lines of his hand. But he liked the way it felt against his skin, and through his pondering concluded that a wedding ring could never truly be poor because it was a symbol of eternal love—for a circle had no end and *the promise of forever* was the richest gift a person could give. The form—ivory loop, gold band, diamond setting—didn't matter: it was about the love behind it. But adding a diamond provided an indestructible symbol to the band—that was what the Greek root of the word *adamas* meant —*indestructible*—for nothing could cut a diamond except itself, and the poor ring needed a stone he thought. He fell asleep with marriage on the bow of his mind as he pushed off into the dark dreamscape.

5

Teddy splashed the cold water on his face and ran it through his hair. He set the metal pail underneath the outside barn spigot, allowing it to fill. Last night's dream lingered in the window of his mind like water drops waiting to evaporate.

During this dream, for the first time, he hadn't been on the ship but in a clearing of sage grass next to a soft wheat field. The land rolled across the horizon and fell down rocky cliffs into a turquoise sea of small wooden fishing boats. He lay in the grass with a Spanish woman dressed in white. She wrapped her arm around his chest, and when he leaned his face into her ebony hair, he found it had the scent of a river and her skin smelled like milk. In the distance, there was a modest home in the Spanish style. The dream ended there —it was short, but beautiful.

Watching the water in the pail rise, he felt that same love he felt for Sarah. He rubbed the ache out of the birthmark on his leg, which was in the same spot the canon in the dream landed on his leg, turned off the spigot, and carried the full pail toward the tree house where he saw Cos sleeping shirtless in the hammock outside.

He walked up the stairs and threw the pail of water on his son. Cos sprang forward, drawing a deep breath in shock. His drenched hair mopped down in front of his eyes. Whipping around, he couldn't help smiling when he saw his father.

"Rise and shine, son! Top of the morning!"

"I was having a great dream, and you ruined it!"

"It's nine o'clock, Cosby! Time for you and Jojo to bathe the horses. Afterwards, y'all can get breakfast."

"I am tired. I stayed up too late."

"That's your fault!"

Cos was red-faced and fell back down on the hammock. "Come on, Dad. If I clean the horses *and* the pool later, can I sleep a little longer?"

"No."

Cos closed his eyes and started to drift back to sleep. A shrill ring jacked him up again; he flipped over out of the hammock, landing on his knees on the tree house porch floor.

"I am up, I am up! No more foghorn," Cos said with a very serious look on his face, holding an ear with one hand and pushing forward at Teddy as if to stop traffic with the other. "We won the game and I graduated, can't I have one day off?" he pleaded.

"I know you did, but the horses don't care if you win, lose, or graduate. Jojo is already up."

"Really? Good Lord, what's wrong with him?"

"The foghorn," Teddy said. "He fell asleep on the couch in the living room and I got him early." He giggled like a little boy.

"That explains it."

"How did you end up out here anyway?" Teddy asked.

"I just wanted to sleep in the hammock."

Teddy knelt down next to him and his tone changed. "Look son, I have some bad news. The high school received a phone call about the cow prank yesterday, a janitor who works for the school saw you in plain sight in the chicken mobile, and they called this morning. You get to keep your diploma, but they reported the episode as a disciplinary infraction to the University of Florida. Your full ride there depended on a perfect behavioral record for your third and fourth quarters. The athletic director called this morning to say they still want you to play ball if you pay your way. And there's more: the high school wants you to help pay for the damages."

"Oh no! *What?* I didn't even do anything. I didn't even know what they were doing! I just dropped them off!"

"Don't complain if you fall asleep with dogs and wake up with fleas."

"Aww man. How much do I owe?"

"One thousand dollars. All four of you have to pay that amount," said Teddy.

"*What?* Where I am gonna get that kind of money?"

"You'll find a way," Teddy said. He patted him on the back and stood up, strolling over to the railing of the porch. Leaning his mass on it, he gazed out across the land.

"Can you help me, Dad?"

"No. You can take a loan out for school and work the rest off."

"Dammit. They can't do this to me!"

"They didn't do anything to you. You broke the rules, and it cost the school a lot and was a great inconvenience to a lot of people. What did you expect? I am disappointed and sad for you. This is your mess to clean up," Teddy remarked.

"I understand. I made a mistake."

"You're welcome to stay here for as long as you need. I want you to keep a positive attitude. We can't feel bad enough to make a bad situation better. What do we do when we fall off the horse?" Teddy turned to him.

"Cowboy up," Cos moped.

"Cowboy up, that's right—now get to those horses. Doing some manual chores today will build some good character in you." He turned and headed down the stairs. "God, it's a beautiful day."

Cos stood up and raked his wet hair back. He didn't put on a shirt, but slipped on cowboy boots and made his way to the barn, where he met Joey walking from the house. They greeted and entered the barn. Cos glided over to Caramel, the brown quarter horse, while Joey tended to Vanilla, the white quarter. The scent of manure and dry hay gave Joey a long-forgotten high.

The two washed the horses and then Joey hosed off Vanilla. Afterwards, he handed the hose to Cos, who finished washing off Caramel. Then they both attended to Earful, Teddy's white Arabian.

Cos whistled to Dog, who ran in from patrolling the yard and the two walked back toward Isabella, the Floridian sun tanning their skin. The air was dense with moisture; Joey and Cos stopped by the kitchen to get a drink while Dog went around back.

Charlotte, the Dollarhides' maid, greeted them with her kind eyes. Her blonde hair had white and silver strands through it and her skin looked untouched by the sun. She wiped her hands on her apron and tilted forward to hug Joey. Charlotte was a live-in maid and chef with her own quarters at Isabella.

"Hello sugar, it's been so long since I've seen you."

"Only since Christmas, Charlotte," Joey said.

"Well that's a *loonng* time now. You look so good and healthy."

"Thanks Charlotte! You look great yourself. How old are you now, thirty-two?"

"Oh, stop it Joey, you must be thirsty! Let me get you some fresh lemonade."

"That would be great!" Joey said.

She took out the chilled glass pitcher of lemon juice mixed with water and tupelo honey, poured two glasses and handed them to Cos and Joey. "Thanks Charlotte," Cos said and they both downed their glasses in one long sip and then refilled them from the pitcher. The drink was the perfect remedy to offset the ninety-five-degree scorcher. The boys said goodbye to Charlotte and headed out the twin louvered living room doors to the pool. Making their way to the water's edge, their feet came to an abrupt halt. Joey and Cos stood in front of the pool with an opened mouth; Dog sat beside him, confused.

"What the hell is it?" Joey said.

"Based on the weather dial in the deep end and the missing shed, I am guessing it's the old shed!" said Cos. The floating wood and grime from the former building stained some of the water brown.

"What's the shed doing *in the pool*?" Joey added.

"Beats the hell outta me," Cos added.

"Go tell Charlotte," Joey barked.

"What's it doing in there?" Cos asked.

"Never mind, Cos, just go!" Joey replied.

Cos went to the back porch, opened one of the doors, and yelled, "Charlotte, did ya know the shed is floating in the pool?"

"*What?*"

"Shed is in the pool!"

She walked out wiping her hands on a rag from the kitchen.

"What in the good Lord's name?" Charlotte said, staring out. Then, she placed a hand in front of her mouth.

"What happened, Charlotte? It looks like a tornado hit it," Cos said.

"I wish! That would at least make sense. The maintenance guys were supposed to demolish the old shed and take it off the property this morning. I reckon they accidentally dragged it into the pool," she replied, short of breath, and placed her hand on her chest, tapping it lightly and frowning.

"What idiots," Joey replied.

"Welcome home, Jojo!" Cos said, throwing his arm around his brother and grinning.

"Thanks, Cos," Joey said in a sarcastic tone.

The sound of a pickup truck pulled up the driveway and two hefty men got out and strutted through the gate. Charlotte turned to them, "You boys have a lot of explaining to do!" she said.

"Howdy ma'am, good day." A large blonde named Billy lifted his dirt-stained hat off his head and fitted it back.

"Explain yourselves, right now!" Charlotte demanded.

"Yes ma'am, well, you see, we had a little problem today."

"That's as plain as day," she said as they stopped in front of her.

"After my fellow Bob here got the rope around the structure, my other boy Steve drove it forward, but we was off a little bit in the calculations and it went the other way on us."

"Why didn't you come tell me?"

"Oh, we was going to, but you see, we had to go eat. We

went and done picked up some of that BBQ over yonder at the Big Pit. You should try the pulled pork sandwich with coleslaw," Billy said.

Charlotte's face turned red and she stomped her shoe on the porch, "I don't care about no coleslaw. I wanna know why you haven't gotten it out yet!"

"Well, no offense ma'am, but we figured it ain't going nowhere anytime soon," Bob said, beginning to laugh a little; Billy stepped on his toe hard and he zipped it.

"You see ma'am, Steve's hypoglycemia acts up, and if he don't eat, he can't really think straight. He's liable to Smurf up and pass out on us. It's happened before," Billy said.

"Yes ma'am," Bob confirmed.

"I don't know what to do with y'all." They looked down as she paused. "Just get this mess cleaned up before Mr. Dollarhide gets back."

"Uh, ma'am, that's just the thing. We got a big hunting expedition this afternoon that we've gotta get ready for. We came back just to let cha know."

"Unbelievable! Y'all are dumber than a bag of hammers. I bet if I took both of your heads and rubbed them together it wouldn't make one bright idea," Charlotte said. Cos and Joey tried not to smile.

"We would like to do it ma'am, but this is a real special event. Last week, Will Burns spotted Half Ton on his farm and organized a group hunt for today."

"That's Belle's dad," Joey said, his voice lifting.

"You two should be ashamed of yourselves. Do you fools even know there's a storm coming?"

"Yes ma'am. It's an early hunt. We'll be here a couple of days after the storm to take care of this."

"Well, what choice do I have? You fools won't help me!" Charlotte barked, her face beet red now.

"Who's Half Ton?" Joey asked.

"He's a wild hog running loose in the area. People say he may be the longest ever, weighing *over a thousand pounds,*" Cos said, exaggerating his face and voice.

"Yep, they say he's longer than Hog Kong, that hybrid shot in Kentucky," Bob said, his smile revealing a missing front tooth.

"What do you want with a stupid hog anyway?" Charlotte asked, frustrated.

"He's destroying the landscape and he's dangerous, ma'am. If provoked, he could kill someone," Billy said.

"*And* Will Burns is offering a trophy and a twenty-five thousand-dollar reward to whoever pops him," Bob said; Billy hit him again.

"*Oh*, so this is about money?!"

"Money and pride. We're sorry ma'am, we'll be back though. Y'all take care now." The two headed out the gate and back to their truck.

"Holy smokes!" Joey replied, his eyes big as saucers. "I wanna go!"

"No Joey, you're not going anywhere," Charlotte said.

"Why not? Teddy and I killed a black bear in Montana with my bow back in the day. I could pick off that hog easy enough."

"That's enough, Joey. It's time for breakfast, boys. We'll have it outside, and let's pretend this never happened," Charlotte added. "They're perfect examples of what occurs when you sniff gasoline and drop out of school."

They all sat down on the outside porch at the dining table. Charlotte went inside and came back out, setting the table with a crisp white cloth. They brought out the food, decorating the table with bowls of delicious fruits, sweet cream, tupelo honey, and freshly baked goods. When she finished, Charlotte relaxed into one of the teak chairs and wiped the sweat off her brow. She stared out at the pool, saw the weather dial bobbing with the current, and shook her head again in disgust. The boys sat around shirtless. A white '78 CJ-5 Jeep passed the truck on its way out; it stopped and Wolly hopped out. He had left early to run some errands.

"Did I miss breakfast?" he asked as he swung through the back gate.

"There's not enough. You should've called first," Joey said.

"There's never enough for Boone," Cos said.

"Oh stop it, boys. There's plenty to go around, Wolly," Charlotte said.

"Where's Dad?" Joey asked.

"He's on the back lot," Charlotte replied.

"Pass me the fruit please," Wolly said. Joey passed him a big bowl of organic blueberries and strawberries. Wolly served himself, pouring fresh cream on top.

"I love berries and cream," he exclaimed, adding a heaping spoonful of the tupelo honey to it.

Joey buttered his pancakes and drank a glass of milk. Then, he unloaded some scrambled eggs onto the plate, along with a cut tomato.

"Thank you for joining us this morning, Wolly," Charlotte added.

"No—thank you, Charlotte, for all this good food."

"How did graduation go?" Charlotte asked.

"Really great, Charlotte," Cos said.

"Yeah, it went great!" Wolly said.

"Your dad told me you lost your scholarship, Cosby," she said, looking at him with the concerned eyes of a mother. After they lost Sarah to cancer six years ago, Charlotte took over the role and had shared in their successes and failures ever since.

"Yes, it's true." He darted his eyes down, deflated.

"What?" Wolly said, looking at Cos.

"Florida found out about the prank and cut my scholarship," Cos stated. Wolly's eyebrows pointed up—Cos shook his head in the negation, indicating they didn't know about Wolly—Joey looked shocked.

"Oh, you boys didn't know. I am sorry," Charlotte remarked.

"No, I didn't know. That's terrible," Joey said. Cos shrugged.

"Well, I want you to stay positive. You'll get through this," Charlotte remarked.

"Thanks, Charlotte."

"Y'all know the weather channel says Hurricane Eliza will be here early tomorrow morning," Charlotte said.

"I know. There's a little get-together on the beach after dinner," Joey said.

"Well, I certainly *don't* want y'all going to that."

"But Charlotte," Cos said. "*Everyone* in our class will be there."

"He means *Leslie* will be there," Wolly said with a grin.

"Shut up, Boone!" Cos said.

"It's just up the road. I'll keep an eye on him," Joey said to Charlotte.

"All right—you can go, but be *very careful*, and watch out for the weather. If it starts to rain, head straight home."

"We will," Joey said.

A loud vehicle barreled up the driveway. Through the opened gate, they saw a camouflaged fire truck pass by. In a moment, a man with a strong build and a belly hanging out over his dirt-stained Levi's lumbered into the backyard, his weight shifting back and forth on the heels of his ostrich-skin cowboy boots.

"Howdy folks! Name is Bob Barclay. I am here to see about some limbs that need cutting."

"Nice to meet you, Bob. Mr. Dollarhide has been expecting you. He should be up here any minute."

"All right, thank you. I'll take a look while I wait." He exited.

After ten minutes, Teddy came around the side where the camouflaged fire truck surprised him. Bob surveyed a tree with his hands on his hips. Seeing Teddy approach, he turned with his hand out.

"Howdy sir. Bob Barclay! You must be Teddy."

"Hi Bob. Nice to meet you." Teddy noticed a protruding bulge two inches off his forehead.

"Don't let the knot get to you."

"Didn't even see it."

"Still getting used to it. I was climbing a coconut palm last year to get a lady's black cat out, and that damn cat knocked loose a big nut with its hind leg that hit me square in between the eyes. The shot knocked me off the tree and I landed on the ground unconscious. When I woke, I had this knot, and it's been with me ever since."

"That's the damnedest thing I've ever heard, Bob."

"Yeah, at first I thought it was one of those chupacabras, but it was just a cat. But that cat had it out for me. They tell you don't cross a black cat's path, but there ain't nothing about not getting in a tree with one," Bob said and laughed. "That ain't even the half of it. Ever since I went out, I've had selective tel-e-pathy."

"You mean you can see into the future?"

"Yep, I can predict the weather one day in advance." He held a finger up in the air. "I tried to get on the weather channel with it, but they said it wasn't scientific enough, whatever the hell that means. I listen to them enough to know their batting average is low."

"So tell me, do you think Eliza will be big?"

"Big *and* early!"

"Weatherman has it here around 2:30 am."

"Naw, it'll be sooner."

"I hope you're wrong."

"There are two things I am never wrong about, Mr. Dollarhide: trees and weather."

"But *no one* is right *all* the time, Bob," Teddy said, smiling.

"I suppose you're right. The truth is I don't want this telepathy. Hell, it's a burden knowing what the weather will be. I can't tell you how many fishing trips I've canceled. I even visited a head specialist to see if he could fix it. He told me he could polish the knot down, but couldn't rid me of the mind stuff."

"So you decided to keep the knot?"

"Yeah, I kinda like it. It's a good reminder to avoid things like black cats, walking under ladders, and the number thirteen, because *those* things are *real*."

"Now I don't know about all that."

"No, they're as real as anything else."

"Well I have different colored horses, and they're all the same."

"But a horse isn't a cat, Mr. Dollarhide."

"No, but a cat has as much color to him as a horse or a flower or any other thing."

"Sounds like French to me. You get tangled up with the cats then; I'm staying away from them."

"Let's get back to talking trees, Bob. The day isn't young

and I want these weak limbs trimmed before the storm so the wind can't hurl them at us."

"All right, what have we got here?"

"I'll show you."

They walked around the property and Teddy pointed out weak limbs in trees.

"I want these gone before the storm. Can you do it by this afternoon?"

Bob paused for a moment to reflect, squinting to the side as he took his Florida Gators ball cap off and wiped the sweat from his forehead with a handkerchief from his front pocket.

"Oh, I reckon my crew can start right now and be finished by this afternoon. There's a hunt on Will Burns's land for Half Ton around four o'clock, so we got to be done by three."

"For the feral hog?"

"Yessiree. He's no longer staying at the Willis Plantation. Will Burns saw him on his farm in the country a good five miles closer to town. Miss Jimmy lives next door and claims he snuck in her yard at night and cleared out the chickens. Ate 'em whole, beak and all. Damn thing is possessed by Satan himself."

"I am not sure if I buy all that."

Bob's face curled up. "No, it's true. He's got the mark of the beast and needs to be stopped before he kills somebody."

"Okay, well, please get to these trees and let me know when you're done."

"Remember, Eliza will be big and early!" he said, and walked away.

"Gotcha, Bob."

Teddy walked to the backyard. Meanwhile, Bob moved

the camouflaged firetruck onto the grass near the trees. The country group Alabama's "Song of the South" began to pour out of a loudspeaker mounted on the top of the firetruck. Bob raised a ladder attached to the top; he and the crew started working. The music stopped Teddy at the door to the preservation room, where he watched the spectacle for a moment. Then, he went inside, retrieved the antique pistol, and joined the group in the backyard.

"I see the gang's all here. How's breakfast?" Teddy said, glimpsing the pool out of one eye. "What happened here?"

"The guys you hired to remove the shed dragged it *into* the pool!" Charlotte said.

"How did that happen?"

"They said it 'went the wrong way on them' when they pulled it," Charlotte said. Teddy scratched his head, staring at the pool perplexed.

"Why didn't they remove it?" He turned and looked at Charlotte.

"Said they had to go eat."

"Will they be here later on?"

"Nope, they're going hunting for that hog." With each answer, Teddy became more and more astonished.

"That's bull. They're fired! I'll get Bob to do it." He walked over, sat down at the table, and rested the pistol on the tablecloth to the side of his empty plate.

"How's the food, Wolly?" Teddy said, patting him on the back.

"Excellent, sir."

"What's that music, Dad?" Joey asked.

"Oh, that's the tree man." He picked up a piece of toast.

"Does he make you pay extra for that?" Joey asked.

"No, it's a free perk. Fortunately, it's Alabama, so I can't really complain."

"Who is this guy?" Charlotte asked.

"Bob Barclay." Teddy filled a bowl with fruit, poured cream on top of it, and then served himself a coffee. "Is this Jamaican Blue Mountain?" he asked Charlotte.

"Yep!"

"My favorite. You're an angel, Charlotte," Teddy said. "I gotta tell y'all something," Teddy said, beginning to laugh. "Bob just told me that he's telepathic."

"What?" Joey said.

"Yeah, a cat hit him in the head with a coconut and he can see into the future."

"The day just keeps get weirder. Did you bring in something strange with that cannon?" Charlotte asked.

"Maybe." Teddy smiled. "He tells me he can predict the weather one day in advance and promised me Eliza will come early and be really big."

"You're not gonna listen to him, Dad?" Joey asked.

"Not really, but I want y'all to board up everything right now, every window except for the kitchen bay window."

"You got it," Cos said.

"Why leave it uncovered?" Wolly asked.

"It's impact-proof glass, and I like to have a lookout during storms," Teddy said. "And come home early tonight from that beach party. I think Bob just might be onto something."

"Okay," Joey and Cos answered.

Cos noticed the gun. "The pistol looks great cleaned up."

Teddy held it up, admiring it. "Thanks, still waiting for Patch to put a date on it, but the model was a popular one when *La Gracia* sank."

"Sweet," Joey said.

"Check out the engraving," Teddy said and passed it to Cos, who studied it.

From what they could make out, the whole body was engraved with intricate patterned lines.

"What a nice piece. They sure don't make 'em like they used to," Cos said.

"No they don't," Teddy said as Cos handed it to Joey.

"What's this?" Joey asked as he flipped out a small octagonal piece that resembled an Allen wrench from the handle; there was a hexagonal hole at the end of it.

"It's a belt tie, although I've never seen one like this."

"Hmm," Joey said.

"So what's the tale on the gun, Jojo?" asked Teddy, grinning.

"A very poor servant stole it from his master along with some bread and ran away to assassinate a man for a hefty sum. Got wet feet, and practically gave it away at the docks to a sailor."

"That's pretty good. Cos?" Joey passed the pistol back to Cos, who studied it.

"It was a vanity pistol for a rich nobleman. Only been shot once, virtually by accident, when his right-hand man was showing him how. The rogue shot hit his horse in the butt and his servants laughed at him; he had them punished in an embarrassing fashion and the pistol was thrown away in disgust, only to be retrieved by a future cook on *La Gracia*."

"Very, very good Cos; I am impressed," Teddy said.

"Thanks."

"Charlotte?" Teddy asked as Cos passed the gun her way.

"Oh, this is a stupid game, you know how I hate guns." She hurried it to Wolly, holding it with two pinched fingers by the handle like a dirty sock.

"Wolly?" Teddy asked. Wolly looked at it for a minute.

"Not sure Salt, probably went to battle, did well, and the same man was a sailor when the war ended." He passed it back to Teddy.

"What do you think, Salt?" Wolly asked. Teddy paused, studying it.

"I think it was an orphan, owned by no man, created as a humble servant, a masterless sailor on a ride to the New World to find its one true owner, but it ran into a bullet-proof foe who threw it to the bottom of the ocean where it has waited patiently for hundreds of years to fulfill its destiny."

"I like that, Salt. So, has it found its owner and destiny yet?" Wolly asked.

"Must have, because its destiny is now in our hands." He set the pistol down and leaned back in the chair. "So, what else is new, boys?"

"Joey is in love," Cos said.

"Really? *You too?*" Teddy said, smiling and winking at Cos. Joey turned red and shook his head with a grin. "So what does love look like?"

"Redheaded like a firecracker," Wolly said, laughing.

"Shut up, Wol," Joey barked. Teddy laughed. "Oh now Wolly, redheads are the salt of the earth. My wife was a redhead."

They talked for another half hour and dispersed with full bellies.

Out in the yard, Barclay continued to work the trees, using a ladder attached to the top of the firetruck to reach and saw off half-broken and weak branches and limbs while his team cut the fallen pieces down to size, throwing them into the bed of a grey Dodge Ram pickup truck belonging to one of the three crewmen, who just happened to be Buzz Smith, Leslie's ex-boyfriend.

After Bob finished hours later, he handed Teddy an invoice. Teddy went inside to get his checkbook.

In the office, his heart sank when he saw his checking balance. A stack of unpaid bills sat on the broad pine desk. He put his fingers on his temple, which throbbed with his heartbeat. He walked out to Bob with his checkbook in his hand and asked him if he would remove the shed from the pool. Bob agreed, quoting him a price for that. Teddy added it to the tree removal total, wrote the man a check and handed it to him. Then, Teddy went back to the office and sat down to thumb through the bills he had been avoiding. He started with the five maxed out credit cards; he could barely meet the minimums. Then, he came to a letter marked IMPORTANT in red. Opening it, he read the notice, detailing his debt on one year of back property taxes on Isabella. Unlike his other notices, this one gave him an ulti-matum of thirty-five days to pay a huge minimum he couldn't afford before the state seized the property. Making a paper airplane out of the letter, he glided it toward the trash can—it bounced off the top of the pile of other airplanes like it, ricocheted off the wall, and landed behind the desk. He jolted up, pushed the chair back, and rested his forearm on the doorframe, pushing his forehead into it. His eye caught his plans for the wooden sailing boat he wanted to build, tacked to the wall. Next to it hung a map of Florida and the Caribbean; a highlighted route ran from the coast of Latch to St. Barts. Around the map, his drawings of dreams from *La Gracia* lined the walls. Closing his eyes, he envi-sioned being on the boat, sailing off into the horizon, wearing his aviators with Bear by his side. After a moment, he regained his composure and ran his fingers through his hair and beard; then, he went out to the porch.

The boys spent the rest of the afternoon boarding up the

windows on Isabella, while Teddy loaded *Gold Lip* at the marina and took the boat to a warehouse inland, which always charged a handsome fee to board boats during storms.

The boys placed the chickens in the second floor area of the barn, which Teddy had specifically built for use during bad storms, and penned them up. They didn't anticipate flooding, so they left the horses and the zebu bull downstairs in their stalls which was generally better for any spin-off twisters so long as there was no significant surge. Afterward, Cos returned the chicken car to Dan's, about three miles south and two miles inland; Joey gave him a ride back.

6

About every fifty yards, a wooden bridge crossed over big dunes that descended to the white beach along the east side of Route 1. At the center of every bridge, there was a beehive-shaped gazebo with wooden benches inside. Cars and trucks lined the side of the dark road and the full white moon shimmered on the black ocean. A strong breeze cooled the eighty-eight-degree night, sending sand dancing across the road. The moist air told of an approaching storm.

Joey, Wolly, and Cos walked over from Isabella wearing T-shirts, chinos, and cologne, Dog trailing behind them. They took the main bridge down to the campfire. A gang of seniors ran past them, carrying a six-pack of beer, their weight drumming the wooden boards. Young ladies ahead in "beach formal" attire chatted about their summer and college plans. Lavender and white rose oil from their perfume lingered in the air, and when the boys passed through it, they experienced the essence of June.

A sea of floral, white, and pastel hues colored the sand. They slipped their shoes off and walked past the fire, which whistled smoke in the air. A crowd was gathered around it, sitting on driftwood logs and folding chairs. A senior named Jesse, a black guy with short knotty dreads, sang along to his acoustic guitar. Guys and girls chatted together in circles outside of the fire, recollecting about the past four years. Joey saw his old friend Jackson sitting on a Yeti cooler like a guard dog and told Wolly and Cos he would retrieve the beers and catch up with them; Wolly slipped him a roll of cash for a six-pack.

Joey paid Jackson for two six-packs of Sweetwater Georgia Brown. He noticed Buzz Smith at the bonfire, glaring at Cos. Wolly and Cos caught up with some old buddies behind him and Joey joined them, handing a six-pack to Wolly.

In a circle next to them, Belle and Paige socialized with Leslie and Belle's friend Natasha. Natasha had gone to a neighboring high school in Mangotan up north and had roomed with Belle during her freshman year at the University of Texas. Her brown hair was pulled behind one ear; she had round cheeks and a tiny mouth with thick lips—the top lip hung over the bottom one, furling up when she spoke. An assembly of guys came and went trying to get her number—the harder they tried, the more she lost interest.

Belle stood next to her. Baby blue and canary outlines of flowers climbed her cream dress and a new Hawaiian Plumeria was tucked behind her ear. The eye patch was gone; a bluish and black bruise from the boomerang injury covered the area near her nose, and the white of her left blue eye was a little red. Joey walked over to them, and Wolly and Cos followed. Dog ran up to the ladies, recognizing them from the day before.

"Hey Joey, hey Cosby; I want you to meet our friend Natasha! She was my roommate freshman year," Belle said.

Joey fist bumped Natasha, smiling. "Nice to see you again," he said.

"You too," she said.

"Great seeing you," Cos said, fist bumping her next.

"Thanks Cosby," Natasha said.

"Hey Dog!" Belle said.

"Oh, look at how cute he is!" said Natasha, petting him. Even Dog took to Natasha, putting his paws up on her dress.

"Get down, baby. I just got this dress," she said, pushing him down and brushing off the cotton knit.

The girls poured affection on him and he shook his body sideways in approval, wagging his stub tail.

"Dog likes the ladies," Wolly greeted them. "Beers?" He extended one to Paige and they each nodded yes. He handed each one a beer.

"Hey babe," Paige added. "Do you know Belle and my friend Natasha?"

"No, I don't think so, how do you do?" Wolly asked, tipping his ball cap to Natasha.

"Good, thanks," Natasha replied.

"So, what did y'all do last night?" Paige asked.

"Went swimming and ate a bushel with Old Salt. A perfect night," Wolly said.

"Sounds like a good time," Paige added. "How about this hurricane?"

"I can't believe this many people showed up tonight. A lot of people evacuated," Leslie said.

"We *always* stay. Teddy makes us," Joey said.

"Yeah, but your house is a fortress!" Leslie said.

"Leslie was just telling us about how incredible it is. Why haven't I ever gotten to see it?" asked Belle, looking at Joey.

"I don't know. You should come by sometime. It's a

castle," Joey said and looked at Belle. Now that he could see into both eyes, he was in the deep end again and he never wanted to leave.

"That'd be great." She smiled at him, and then they both looked back at the others.

"It sounds great," Natasha said. She gave a pleasing smile whenever she glanced at Joey, while messing with her hair. He noticed and, on any other occasion, would have been very flattered.

"Count me in," Leslie said.

"You're in," Cos said, and she smiled.

"Y'all be careful! As we were leaving, the news reported Eliza is a Cat 2!" Paige said.

"Yeah, we heard," Cos said.

"This storm is going to be really rough if you're close to the ocean, even in your house. Dad has us booked at the Holiday Inn twenty miles inland so we're nowhere near the water," Wolly said.

"I hope my cousin's wedding in Savannah isn't canceled this weekend," Natasha said.

"Oh, consider it canceled," Wolly said. "I am surprised it isn't already raining here."

"Yeah, me too," Paige added.

"If everyone just hunkers down, I am sure it'll be all right, though." Wolly swigged his Georgia Brown and looked around. "Hey, is there any food here?"

"I think Zach has some hot dogs over at the bonfire," Paige said.

Wolly remarked, "Oh baby, I love a dog cooked over an open flame."

"I'll go with you. Come on!" Paige took him by the arm and they exited.

"Leslie told me about the pistol Cos found. It sounds so

interesting. I wondered how his search was going this year," Belle said.

"Thanks. Yeah, Dad fished a baseless cannon out and feels he may be really close to something big. That means he's close to finding the hull, probably," Joey said.

"Did he let you see the cannon?" Belle said, smiling.

"Yeah, he lets us see everything," replied Joey.

"How neat," Belle said.

"I am sure he would be willing to take y'all out on *Gold Lip* one day if you want to come along," Cos added, fishing for Joey. Joey didn't appreciate it but stayed quiet.

"We'd love that, *wouldn't we* Leslie?" Belle said, looking at her.

"Oh yeah, Teddy is a great guy to! You'll like him, Belle."

"It's a deal. I already have my diving license," Belle said.

"Do you really?" Joey asked.

"Yep, I love to dive."

"We'll go then," Joey said.

"I wanna go," Natasha said.

"Sure," Joey said to her.

Jesse started to play Dave Matthews's "Me and You" in the background. "I love this song," Cos said. "Why don't we all go over and sit by the fire?"

"Sounds good, it's hard to pass on some Dave," Joey said.

They headed over. Joey managed to find his way next to Belle, who sat next to Paige, who leaned into Wolly, who was now working on his second hot dog. Natasha plopped down on the other side of Joey. Natasha and Joey talked and she asked him about school and life. After a while, she stretched out her legs, pushing her feet into the sand; her legs shining from the light of the fire. Jesse finished the song and transitioned into a Van Morrison song reminiscent of John Lee Hooker.

Leslie and Cos sat behind everyone with Dog; Cos rubbed her back; Dog managed to knock over an abandoned Sweetwater on a plastic trash bag and licked it up; Buzz sat across the bonfire, watching Cos and Leslie with a hot grimace. Seeing him, Cos decided they should go.

"I want to throw the ball for Dog in the ocean. You wanna come?" said Cos.

"Sure!" said Leslie.

"Come on then."

They got up and headed north along the water. Dozens of crabs skated sideways in front of them. Buzz stood up and shook his head, stomping off the other way.

When they neared the water's edge far from the crowd, Cos hurled a ball and Dog ran after it, diving into the black tide. He fished it out and jetted back with his tail wagging. Leslie threw it and he retrieved it again; they laughed at him trampling the waves. Cos tossed it again and took a big swig of his beer.

"He's having too much fun. I can't take it any longer, I am getting in too." He removed his shirt.

"What? Are you crazy? It's dark out and you can't see anything!"

"Can't help it babe, I got saltwater in my veins. Besides, there's nothing but flounder and crabs anyway out there. C'mon in! Can you wade out a little with your arm?" He got in with his chino shorts.

"Kind of. If I get in trouble, can you help me? I have my bathing suit on under my dress."

"I got you; we'll stay shallow."

Leslie finished off her beer and neatly folded her dress, placing it on the dune hill and waded in. They were out of view from the crowd, except for Dog, who sat patiently on the shore, watching them in confusion. Cos splashed her and she splashed back. He splashed harder and she splashed even harder. They both laughed and he tackled her into the warm sea. Their bodies connected in the sand with the tide coming into them, forcing his body into hers. He looked at her, hooking his arms under body.

"What are you doing, Cosby Dollarhide?" she said.

"Getting to know you better," he said with a slight smile.

"Uh-huh!" she said. His lips touched hers, and after some passionate kissing, he rose and helped her back up. They saw Dog running down the coast with Cos' shirt in his mouth. Cos called after him, but he kept going, eventually stopping to dig a hole and bury the shirt. They laughed it off and Leslie and Cos waded out past the second burst of waves. She braced herself on his soft hands.

He braced her and his nose touched her neckline where the jasmine and teak from her perfume mixed with the musk of the ocean. Her wet hand gripped around his neck and they kissed under the moonlight with salty lips. She wrapped her strong legs around his body and pushed her calves down on his butt, bringing his frame closer. In her hazel eyes, he saw a kindness in her heart that stirred his attraction. They kissed for minutes until she stopped him and leaned her head back, soaking her hair in the water; they bobbed in the ocean while he pointed to different constellations.

Back at the fire, Natasha got looser with Joey as she finished her second beer. She kept pushing her leg into his. Waiting long enough to not offend her, he excused himself. Strolling up the coast, Joey passed Dog sitting on top of the covered hole, saw the lovers in the water, and grinned. He kept walking and sat on the sand at the base of a dune where no one could see him.

After about ten minutes, Belle came that way, carrying her shoes.

"Hey Red!" Joey said. She stopped in front of him and looked around.

"Who's that?" Belle asked.

"It's me, Joey!" he said.

"Oh hey Joey, we wondered where you went."

"I just had to get away from the crowd."

"Yeah, me too. Would you like to walk with me?" Belle asked.

"Sure," he replied, hopping up and brushing the sand off his butt before meeting her. They walked along the beach, both carrying a Sweetwater beer.

"Natasha wondered where you went," Belle said.

"Oh yeah."

"Yeah, she really likes you. She told me so."

"That's flattering. I mean, she seems like a great girl," Joey said.

"Most guys fall to pieces when Natasha pays them that much attention. It seems like you ran away from her."

"She's just not my type, really."

"Well, you're the first," Belle said.

They both smiled and paused. They were a little nervous, but glad to be alone. Belle had trouble staring at his eyes without disappearing, and he couldn't stop looking at her lips, which spanned her wide awkward mouth.

They traveled into the black mystery where only the galaxy lit the sand, and then further away still from the flickering fire and the lights of the marina dotting the bay in the distance. They hugged the edge of the tide; the moist sand felt good on their bare feet as the saltwater curled around their toes. Belle savored the caramel malt.

"So, Austin has been great?" Joey asked.

"Yeah. I've met so many good friends and it's a city with a lot of flavor."

"It does have flavor," Joey said.

"It has some of the best BBQ. It's *so* good!"

"I know, Cos and I went to the Rub there once," Joey said and sipped his beer.

"I practically *live* at the Rub!"

"It's so good," he said, and paused. "So, are you dating anyone now?"

"Not at the moment. I just broke up with TJ this spring."

"I am sorry to hear it," he said, his voice almost soaring.

"It's all right. It was long overdue."

"What about you? Is there a *California* girl out there?

"Not right now."

"You've left LA, right?"

"Yeah."

"So no more baseball?"

"Nope. My injury last year cooked my chances at the pros."

"When you ran into the duck?" she said, smiling.

"Yep."

She laughed and tried to stop herself.

"You saw the video?"

"Yes, I tried not to laugh. On the phone you didn't tell me it was from running into a mascot—you said it was from a surfing accident."

"I lied. Actually, ESPN might pay me to do an ad." He smiled.

"Well at least something good will come out of it. Did you ever get the girl's number?"

"No, she won't speak to me," Joey insisted.

"Aww, I am sorry."

"It's okay, but I'll take the sympathy."

"Wasn't it your dream to play in the majors?"

"Growing up, it was always ball, but my dreams changed when I got hurt," he said, and paused.

"My dream has always been to go to Stanford; so far, nothing has changed that." They kept strolling.

"Congratulations, by the way. Stanford Business—that's *impressive.*"

"Thanks."

"Are you excited?" he said as they continued down the beach.

"I am *really* excited, but the truth is my father wants me to go to business school at Texas, and he won't pay for me to go anywhere else unless it's a state school in the Southeastern Conference. If I go to Stanford, he won't even give me a *dime* for living expenses, which would make it very difficult because I would have to work. I don't want to disappoint him, but I also want to be true to myself."

"Bummer," he said. They kept walking.

"What would you do?" she asked.

"I'd follow my heart. If your heart is at Stanford, that's where you have to go. Besides, it's one of the best schools in the country. You can take out student loans and pay them back later on. Plus, northern California has incredible hiking, surfing and skiing."

"Thanks—I think you're right. I already gave my decision, but wasn't sure I'd go through with it. I haven't told my dad yet. I like the sound of all that nature. I am a nature buff myself."

"Underneath the stilettos and expensive purses?"

"I got a couple of boots and a compound bow in my closet."

"Yeah, I bet they have a lot of dust on them."

"*No,* but they got some dried mud on them!" she countered, gauging his response.

He looked smug with humorous disbelief.

"You don't believe me?" she said.

He smiled, "Not for a minute."

"I am more mountain than you, *city boy.*"

"You wanna bet?"

"Yeah, I bet you can't skin a buck with a pocketknife," she said.

"So, you can't either!"

"Can so."

"Well, I'll have to see that sometime. I'll take you hunting this winter."

"No, I'll take you hunting!" Belle snapped back.

"Okay, but I choose the location."

"I'll bring my bow," Belle said.

"I'll bring my pocket knife."

They shook hands, smiling, and walked silently for a moment, still grinning.

"You're full of surprises, Belle. All these years and I never knew you hunted."

"Well there's a lot of things about me that you don't know, Mr. Dollarhide," she said, smiling. He watched the water—she watched the sand. They came across a cluster of trash and she picked it up.

"What the hell?" she said.

"It's a trashball. They wash up in LA sometimes. People need to be much more mindful of water pollution. It's so terrible to mess up your own living space," Joey said.

"Don't shit where you sleep!"

Joey stopped, "Damn! A buck-hunting, cursing nature buff who wears high heels."

"*What?* It sums it up nicely."

"I swear you're the only girl in Latch who thinks like this," Joey said.

"Is that a good thing?"

"It's a great thing."

"Then you must be the only guy in Latch who likes the way I think," she remarked, showing her teeth.

"I doubt that. There's certainly no one as special as you in Latch."

"So I am special now?" Belle said.

"You're *all right*," he said, looking away, trying to hold a straight face. She hit him on the arm and he stopped and turned toward her.

"You know I am joking," he said, and moved closer to her. "Actually, we're a lot alike." He took her beer and set their beers down, then took both of her hands. They ran into each other's eyes and she blushed and glanced down, raised her shoulders, and then looked back up at him with her forehead tilted forward.

"How?"

"Just close," he said. "You know, I've really missed talking to you."

"You should've called," she said, looking at him.

They started to kiss, but a gust of wind blew her red hair to the side of her face and a string landed in front of her lip. The wind carried the white plumeria flower of Kauai from her ear, tossing it back on the sand a few feet away. Joey went over and picked it up and smelled it; watching him, she smiled.

"I think you dropped something, miss." He reached up, placed it behind her ear again, and gently combed her hair with the inside of his fingertips. Then, he moved his hand slowly down the side of her soft cheek to her mouth, where he pulled her bottom lip down. She closed her eyes with her mouth hanging open. When their lips touched, lightning beamed down his body to the end of his toes. He pulled her tight and their mouths interlocked with their tongues dancing together in a perfect two-step. Her breath was sweet and he could still taste a touch of the Sweetwater there. A fire burst between them and the wind howled around, blowing her hair over his face; he smelled the jojoba oil in the bristles and the Bulgarian rose oil across her neckline; the wind picked up; warm raindrops fell. He pulled her head gently forward, kissing her on the forehead. She closed her eyes in an attempt to capture the moment, then looked back up at him intensely.

"That was wonderful," she said underneath her breath. Rain began to hit her face and a big drop landed on the tip of her nose.

"You have a raindrop on the tip of your nose," he said, wiping the drop away slowly. "And you're so beautiful."

She smiled. "Even with the black eye?"

"Even through the black eye."

"If you can like me like this, I think you could like me any way."

"I know I would like you any way."

They kissed again and the rain fell harder, soaking their hair. They stopped.

"Oh my God, it's raining cats and dogs!" Belle said, holding her hands up, smiling.

"It sure is! Bob Barclay was right! We better get back. We're pretty far from the bridge. Let's go!" He took her hand and they ran toward the flickering fire in the distance.

Cos and Leslie moved in from the ocean when the rain started; Belle and Joey met them on the beach where Dog looked confused and afraid. Dog made his way ahead of them.

"Where is your shirt Cosby?" Joey asked.

"Somewhere over there, Dog buried them or something!" Cos answered.

"You two are crazy, but I like it," Belle said.

"Come on, we gotta get out of here," Joey said, leading the way.

Sideways rain battered the sand. In the distance, they could see the crowd at the campfire clearing out after dumping big gallons of water on the fire, leaving a pile of smoking ashes and black logs. People made their way off the bridge to their cars. Zach Watts, Leslie's ride, was waiting for her, but Buzz told him she got another ride, so he left. The group arrived at the bridge in five minutes and ran up the slick steps where a ranger stood.

"Do y'all idiots know there's a big ole hurricane coming? You better get on home," the park ranger who had arrived to clear people off the beaches said with a raised voice over the weather.

"Where's Natasha? She's my ride!" Belle yelled, looking around.

"Where's Paige and Wolly?" Cos exclaimed.

"They must have gone home, thinking Leslie could take us back," Belle said.

"No, Zach gave me a ride and he was supposed to wait for me!" Leslie exclaimed loudly through the wind.

"I bet Buzz told him to leave to punish us because he saw us together," Cos said.

"He wouldn't do that," Leslie snapped back.

"I think you overestimate Buzz's generosity," Cos barked through the rain.

"Look, you can come back to our house. It's stucco over masonry, and we have a generator. It's just up the road," Joey said.

"I guess my father can pick me up there. Okay!" Belle yelled through the storm.

"Sounds good," Leslie said.

The rain drenched them as they sprinted across the empty street. Cos had to carry Dog, who was shaking because he was so afraid of the rain. They ran north, hooking a left on Orange Street. On their way to Windswept, the heavens cried; their tears hurt. The group barely saw the path ahead, but managed to find the farm, open the gate, and jog down the long avenue of palm trees, which bent like asparagus in the wind, the leaves blowing sideways. The warm rain on the hot earth created a light haze, and the uplights on the palms still glowed through the sheets of water. They made it to the mahogany door. When they entered, the wind took the door so strongly that Cos and Joey together had to pull hard to shut it.

7

W ater dripped from their clothes and pooled on the clay tiles. Charlotte brought towels and spare clothes for everyone. They took turns changing in the sitting room off the foyer, then Joey led them into the grand den. The rain hammered the roof like a stampede of horses going to battle.

Oversized brandy-colored sofas floated in the den at angles to one another; high-backed leather reading chairs sat to the side of them. A coquina stone mantel commanded the wall facing the back porch, and a painting of a wizened man on a bald hillside hung above it. An antique Persian rug carpeted the mahogany floors running underneath the sofas. Animal skins, paintings, photos, and antiques climbed the fifteen-foot walls like ivy. The aroma of rolling tobacco and rich leather saturated the room, while sandalwood oil dispersed from a diffuser in the corner in cycles. A white sheet covered a baby grand piano crowded in another corner of the low-lit room.

The group flopped down on the couches; Dog took a spot on the floor next to Bear. The ladies walked around the room. In a minute, Charlotte entered wearing a crisp white button-up and a long grey skirt; she leaned forward slightly with her hands in front as she walked.

"Oh, you sweet things are all wet and cold. Come sit down and let me get you some hot coffee and tea. This hurricane is like an uninvited guest that topped it off by showing up early. Better call your parents and tell them you'll wait it out here. It'll blow all night."

"Oh, I can't stay, I have to get home!" Belle said. "My parents will worry."

"Me too," Leslie said.

"But ladies, you could get hurt going out in this. We can't have that. Y'all can call them and tell them you'll stay here. It's what's best."

"But..." Belle protested.

"I won't hear it. Isabella has masonry in her walls. Now, you just sit right here and make yourself at home." Charlotte's voice was like melted caramel seducing Belle into agreement.

"The house is that safe?" Belle asked.

"Yes, sugar," Charlotte answered.

"It'll be fine," Leslie said to Belle.

"Okay, I'll call them," Belle said.

"Oh good," Charlotte said.

Leslie called her parents also. She smacked on a big piece of gum, blowing bubbles and popping them quick, her way of dealing with the stress. Teddy walked in with Blue on his shoulder and greeted them. They laughed at the sight of the bird. Belle handed Teddy the phone, asking him to explain the situation to her mother. Leslie's parents, on the other hand, were okay with the arrangement and didn't need to speak to Teddy.

"Sure," he said, taking the phone to speak to Belle's

mother. "Well, they were at the beach and the storm blew in early. My house is very secure. It has survived all the big ones." He paused. "Yes, *all* the big ones." He paused again. "Well, the foundation raises it off the ground five feet and the interior walls contain masonry. Plus, we're over a hundred yards from the ocean. The worst of the storm won't be here for a while, but the rain and wind are fierce. I could drive them home, but I don't think it's safe." He paused, listening. "Ok, I agree. I'll bring them home first thing in the morning. Take care." Teddy handed Belle the phone, and she said goodbye. When they finished, Teddy spoke, "All right, ladies and gentleman. Most of you know my pet macaw, Blue." He looked at the bird. "Say hello, Blue."

"Hell-o," Blue croaked.

The room chuckled.

"And this is my best friend and business partner, Dallas, he decided to ride out of the storm with us this evening," Teddy said.

Charlotte waved at the group, smiling.

"Hey guys," Dal said, leaning back deep into one of the leather chairs.

"Belle, it's very nice to meet you and to have you in our home. I am sorry it happened under these circumstances, but I do say you make the room brighter."

"Nice to finally meet you too, Mr. Dollarhide. I've known Joey for years."

"Thanks Belle. Leslie, it's a pleasure to see you again."

"You too, Teddy."

"I am afraid I have some bad news. Eliza gained momentum due to the warm waters, and it looks like she'll touch down early and may even be a strong category 2 hurricane. A lot of people headed to the old auditorium in Lankford for shelter."

"A strong Cat 2!" Joey said. "Good grief Dad, that *is* bad news."

"Yeah, but *don't worry,* Isabella is a tank. Nothing can move her. Aside from the library upstairs, this room provides the most protection, so I'd like for y'all to sleep in here tonight. There are quilts for bedding in the closet. Ladies, you're welcome to the couches. Guys, you're sleeping on the floor. Any questions?"

Shaking their heads in the negative, they let the information digest.

"Okay, now that we got that out of the way, we might as well relax. Charlotte, will you please bring in some refreshments?" Teddy asked.

"Certainly," Charlotte replied.

"Thank you." She exited. Teddy went into the connected dining room, where he placed Blue in a cage. The power went out. Blackness blanketed the house. Dog's bark startled them.

"Well, I wasn't expecting that this early," Teddy yelled out. "Don't worry, I just need to flip on the generator." He strolled out to the garage and flipped the switch.

A moment later, Charlotte floated in from the kitchen carrying a silver tray with coffee, liqueur, and Earl Grey tea flanked by cookies and English dessert biscuits. They each approached, taking the warm beverages and sweets back to their places on the sofas. Teddy entered, and Charlotte brought Dal and him warm brandy from the kitchen.

"Thank you, Charlotte," Dal said, admiring her beauty as she glided over to Teddy.

"Thanks, Charlotte," Teddy said, taking a big sip. "Why don't you get yourself one?

"That's all right, I am fine."

"Suit yourself, but there's nothing like a warm brandy with a storm coming."

"All right, maybe just a pinch." She left.

"Eliza sounds bad," Belle remarked.

"Yeah it does," Joey said.

"What do you think, Salt? You have a lot of experience with storms," Dal said.

"I think it's time to dance!"

"Time to dance?" Dal said, smiling.

"Yes, we dance for protection. I grew up in a little town called Goodchance, Alabama, you see, and it was right smack dab in the center of hurricane alley near the Gulf of Mexico, then I lived in Miami and Key West. I've probably got ten 'canes under my belt. Never been hurt because I always dance or do something good beforehand—as a ritual, you know."

He bounced up, grinned, and turned on the stereo; Sam Cooke zoomed out of the speakers and off the walls, drowning out the sound of the rain. For a big man, Teddy jigged and glided across the room with ease, making the ladies giggle and the men grin. Taking Charlotte's hand, he led her up and they danced on the rug. The crowd watched him spin and move her across the den with grace and began to clap along to the music. Dog followed it and barked, while Bear walked alongside him.

After dancing for a few minutes, a noise sounded near the chimney and a yellow thing flew out of the fireplace. They gradually stopped dancing and clapping, and turned to watch the strange visitor. By the way it fell and climbed in the air and its yellow and black coloring, Teddy knew it was an eastern tiger swallowtail butterfly. Their eyes grew wide, their faces filling with wonder.

Dancing around the room, it eventually rested on the coffee table, where it moved its wings up and down.

"Well I'll be. No one has seen a swallowtail here in over a hundred years," Charlotte said.

"Yep, how did he get into the chimney?" Teddy said, pop-eyed.

"Probably just flew in like the birds do," Charlotte said.

They studied him for a moment as Sam Cooke transitioned into "Bring It on Home to Me."

"I think that's our cue," Joey said to Belle. He took her soft hand, and their bare feet crisscrossed the rug. Her long, wet hair was now dark auburn, and as it flipped back and forth, he wished they were alone again. Cos took Leslie's hand and led her around by her one arm. The soul of Sam Cooke insulated the room from the fury of the rising winds outside. Teddy and Charlotte started dancing again after their fascination with the critter wore off. When the song ended, Teddy flopped down in his chair and drank some brandy. They clapped and returned to admiring the stationary butterfly. Bear went after the insect, but Joey batted him down.

Teddy saw another swallowtail flutter out of the chimney. He pointed, "Look, look, another one!" As it danced, they stood in the center of the room watching it ascend above their heads. Another one followed it, and another, and another, and then they kept coming, two and three at a time—a parade waltzing into the room, over fifteen. After a few minutes, they stopped entering, the room full of a dazzling display of pulsing color. Dog barked in excitement and Bear jerked his head this way and that, looking up at them.

"Oh my God! I've never seen anything like this!" Leslie said.

"Where did they come from?" Belle asked.

"They must have sought shelter from the storm in the chimney," Teddy said. "But why they came back after all these years, I haven't got a clue. This is a great blessing, and a good sign for the town."

"You know this town used to be a haven for these butterflies. The eastern tiger swallowtails covered the green spaces by the hundreds—so impressive were the numbers that people would come from as far as Oregon and Michigan to see them. That was before the ... well you know," Dal added.

"Before what?" Belle asked. "I've never heard about this."

"The revolt at the Willis Plantation," Joey said.

"The town secret," Leslie added.

"Now, we don't know that, Joey," Charlotte added.

"Well we know something made that place haunted," Joey said.

"But no one knows what *really* happened. It has never been investigated," Dal added. "Slaves and workers alike just disappeared."

"Whatever! Enough sadness. Tonight is a night of celebration and good cheer before the storm! Let's continue to dance until we're full of it," Teddy said.

"Nothing Can Change This Love" began to play, and the dance partners pulled each other close and swayed in the low-lit room amid the kaleidoscope of butterflies. Some landed on surfaces for a moment, only to start flying again, thirsty for the feeling of the air in their wings. Joey placed his hands around Belle's warm, round hips. They swayed back and forth in the silence of their attraction, still mesmerized by the insects.

Dal took Charlotte's hand and they embraced to the music. They had recently started dating after flirting for years, a slow fruitful harvest of kind words and gestures that erupted into an exhilarating night of sex on the beach after too much Cab Sav and oysters three months ago.

After a while, one of the butterflies landed on Belle's head while she and Joey danced. The group looked on and Leslie commented on it. Belle kept dancing with a grin, allowing it to sit there. The swallowtail spread its wings and then lifted them up again in a fluid motion; its presence tickled her skin, making Joey and her giggle. The song ended and everyone clapped in applause at the show. Belle started to walk, but the butterfly stayed on for the ride.

"He's really taken a liking to you," Dal said with a wide smile. "Joey, I think he's moving in on your girl!"

"What should I do?" she said and held her arms out with the palms up.

"I'll get him," Joey said, attempting to scoop the butterfly up, but it took off, flying across the room in a crooked line until it landed on a metal acorn post of a high-backed chair in the far corner.

The white walls now pulsed with the movement of the black and yellow wings. They took pictures with their phones while Teddy shook his head and smiled before exiting to grab a fishing net and a massive empty aquarium. With the net, he rounded many of them up and placed them in the aquarium that he set on the oversized ebony African coffee table.

Cos exited and returned with piles of quilts that were so old and soft the touch made one want to dive into the fabric, wishing life was always that gentle. Then, he brought down pillows and blankets from the hall closet and handed them to the ladies, who built nests on the deep-lined leather sofas; Cos and Joey spread their blankets on the Persian carpet.

An uncustomary chill filled the house, and Old Salt tossed some logs on the fireplace. Everyone showed concern about there being more butterflies in the chimney, but he shrugged it off, setting the logs ablaze. Charlotte brought in a warm soup made from multicolored heirloom tomatoes and fresh basil picked from the garden. The wind howled outside while they ate the soup and watched the butterflies in the aquarium.

"So, are you excited about college?" Charlotte asked Leslie.

"Yes, I am!"

"I bet your parents will miss you," Charlotte said.

"No. I think they want to get rid of me," Leslie said, laughing and looking at the butterflies, still occasionally tapping on the plastic case.

"Oh, now you *know* that's not true, honey."

"I know, but it *feels* true sometimes."

"Where are you going?" Charlotte asked.

"Miami."

"That's great. What about you, Belle, are you in school now?"

She looked at Joey before turning her head and answering, "I just finished undergrad and I am going to Stanford for business school. At least, I think so."

"That is a very good school! Congratulations!" Teddy said.

"Thank you!" she replied.

Teddy sipped his drink. Thunder clashed. Dog barked.

"*Sit down, Dog!* I swear you're as nervous as a cat's tail in a room full of rocking chairs. I am gonna give him a Benadryl," Charlotte said to Teddy.

"Now Charlotte, you know Dog has a sensitive stomach to everything except wild stuff—last time we gave him a

Benadryl, he farted all night," Teddy said. The room laughed.

"Oh that's right. Well, we can't have him stinking up the place I guess."

"Salt, when do you think the storm will be here?" Dal asked.

"I reckon the eye will be here around one a.m."

"What's the eye?" Colt asked.

"The eye is the worst part," Belle said.

"No, Bellaboo, the eye is the calmest part. It's the center of the hurricane where there's no wind or rain. It's so quiet you can hear a twig break," Leslie said.

"Oh sorry, I was raised inland in Texas, so I am still a hurricane rookie."

"Dad has been in the eye before. Tell them about Key West!" Cos blurted.

"Maybe some other time; I don't want to alarm anyone."

"Aww, c'mon!" Joey said.

"No, next time."

"Teddy, I just love that painting over the mantel," Leslie said.

"Thank you, Leslie." He paused and sipped his drink, studying it.

"That's our super-great-grandpa Luke," Cos said.

"He was a forty-niner out in California during the Gold Rush," Teddy said. "The first gold bug in our family."

"Did he find any?" Leslie asked.

"A little, but he eventually came back to Alabama to be an oysterman and later opened a restaurant."

"Tell us about Luke and the cowgirls!" Cos pleaded.

"Oh, the ladies don't want to hear that," Teddy said.

"What cowgirls?" Belle asked.

"It's a great story! Tell them, Dad!" Joey said.

"Tell us, Salt, *please,*" Leslie begged.

"All right, if you insist." Teddy took another sip of his drink and lit a stogie.

"It was 1853 in the High Sierras of California. Luke and his brother Sam were working a mine for six months and had just struck gold. Life in the mountains was hard. It was frigid at night, and about once a week they tangled with a bear the miners called Ole Sawtooth. Ole Saw was no ordinary bear. It was rumored he weighed seven hundred pounds and had even been shot. Apparently, he had a stomach for gunpowder too; if he could find it in a camp, he would eat it."

"He would eat it?" Leslie asked.

"He *craved it.* One day, Luke found a big sized nugget of gold in the mine and went down to the river to show Sam; Sam was supposed to be panning for gold, but instead he was fishing naked like he used to do." Teddy paused and puffed the cigar, grinning quietly to himself at the thought of Sam. The rain sang outside; he blew some smoke and crossed his legs.

"So, Luke showed Sam the nugget and they decided to go back to the mine about a quarter mile away to celebrate with wine and chocolate, but when they returned, some rough cowgirls with double-barreled rifles and pistol holsters on their belts had seized it. The leader was named Josephine. She was beautiful and had curly red hair. She might have looked gentle, but she was rough, barking orders, drinking whiskey, and spitting on the ground."

Belle's eyes grew big as she listened.

"Luke and Sam had left their guns in the camp, so they didn't know what to do." He paused and sipped his drink again, stroked his white beard, and took another puff off the big cigar. Belle and Leslie leaned forward on the edge of the sofas.

"So *what* did they do?" Belle asked.

"Well, they set up on a high bluff across the river. From there they could see the mine through a hole in the pine trees and juniper brush. Sam suggested a honey burn where a jar of honey is placed in a can and burned on a fire until it boils, producing a white aromatic smoke that sticks to the trees to lure bears to it, so Luke went into town and returned with the honey; they placed it in a can and lit it on a small fire down below. Climbing a nearby tree with a wooden post for hunting, they watched and waited. The burning honey carried a thick white smoke into the air and the pungent aroma blew with the wind, sticking to the bark and leaves. After a little while, Sam hopped down from the tree and picked up the burnt honey. Then, he mixed some molasses with it and ascended the path to the mine camp to paint it on the trees. On his way back, he heard a rumbling in the bush to the left of the path ahead of him."

"What was it?" Leslie asked.

"It's..." Cos started.

"Don't give it away!" Teddy barked. Cos closed his mouth as tight as a keyhole.

Teddy sipped the brandy and dragged his smoke with the whole room waiting. He stood up and paced the room, becoming more exaggerated.

"Out of the bushes, Ole Saw came barreling toward Sam, who dropped the can of honey, running like the wind back to the tree, climbing it faster than a monkey. Saw gunned it straight for the can, licking it with his big pink tongue. Afterward, he waltzed over to the tree and shook it like he was trying to knock a coconut loose. They held on, and after a while, Saw lost interest, choosing to follow the sugary scent into the mine.

"Luke and Sam waited, and about a minute later, they heard a shrill scream that woke the dead—those cowgirls came busting out of the camp half-dressed like they were on fire. So, Luke and Sam went back to the bluff for the night, and lo and behold, when they returned in the morning, Ole Saw was camping out in the shaft," Teddy bellowed. "Damn bear."

"How did they get him out? I forget," Joey asked.

"My dad Jimbo says they went back to town, bought a bow, and did another burn the next night to lead him out into the open, where they shot him. And that's where my bearskin came from." He gestured with his head and eyes to the grizzly skin mounted on the wall; everyone looked.

"It sure is a big skin," Belle said.

"Dad claims that's Ole Saw. Says it's been passed down from Luke. He told us all that nugget of gold sustained him for many years. But you know, getting the truth from him ain't easy," Teddy stated.

"So it could be from another bear?" Belle said.

"Possibly, but a Dollarhide never lets the truth interfere with a good story, you see."

"Thanks Teddy, that's some tale," Leslie said.

"You're very welcome." He sat.

"Legend has it Luke also learned of a John Hodges's treasure up in those mountains, but never found it. Ain't that right Dad?" Joey said.

"Now, I don't know if there even was a treasure; Jim is always spinning a yarn."

"I want to go find it!" Cos said.

"Me too," Belle said.

"If the story is true, Luke looked for it and never found it. What makes y'all think you'll find it?" Teddy said.

"I've got the gold nose, like Dog, you know. Besides, I've got good luck also," Cos said.

"It takes more than luck to find treasure, son," Teddy said. "You need stories and facts, data that hunts."

"Who was John Hodges?" Leslie asked.

"It's been awhile, tell us again Dad," Cos pressed.

Teddy slipped his buffalo-skin moccasins off, rubbing his toes on the Persian wool.

"John Hodges was a sort of legend during the California Gold Rush. He came out West to stake a claim. Legend has it his wife died early of some awful disease. Angry at the world, he became a bandit, assembling a group known as the Triangle of Ghosts who tricked and robbed people all over the West—everyday was Halloween for the Ghosts—but they never killed or hurt anyone, supposedly.

"One day, they cleared a safe of gold out from a bank and headed off into the Sierras to bury it for safekeeping—this way, they could dig it up whenever they wanted, take out whatever they needed, and bury it again. But, while traveling along the road, they happened to be seized by Native Americans, who stole it. They needed it to buy firearms for protection against white soldiers. The Native Americans buried the chest in the mountains until a later date when they planned to cash it in.

"Then what?" Leslie asked, on the edge of her seat still.

"Well about two months later, the Native Americans were attacked before they had a chance to use it. Most were killed, except for a few who fled the area never to return. I suppose that chest remains buried somewhere in the High Sierras to this day, but no one knows where. The Native American told Luke about it in a Bagby jail, I think. Apparently, Luke told the story all the time. Said he went looking for it, but never found anything."

Teddy tugged on his fat cigar, then put it out and finished the drink.

"What a story!" Belle said.

"If it's true, truth sure is stranger than fiction," Teddy said.

"It's a great story, Dad. What do you think about the treasure being there? We should go after it," Cos said.

"I don't know. If you do, be careful—Ole Saw's kin might be roaming around."

A boom occurred outside and everything went black except for the warm glow of the fire. Dog barked. Charlotte rose, reassured the group with her tender voice, and lit some candles, which radiated through the room with a soft blaze. The house started to shake a little from the force of the wind —Joey moved closer to Belle, wrapping his arm around her shoulder—Cos went into the kitchen to get some food— Leslie trailed him.

Teddy and Dal got flashlights to check on the generator while Charlotte continued to cover Isabella in candlelight. When Teddy and Dal reached the garage, the smell of motor oil and burnt metal seeped from the device.

Lightning must have struck the outside convertor, Teddy thought.

In the kitchen, Cos sifted through the counter looking for food; he spotted an apple pie in a glass container. He cut off a fourth of the pie and carried it back to the living room, where Dog was curled up on the ground. Cos entered with the treats and nestled on the sofa next to Leslie—they ate it, sharing a fork.

Charlotte unwound in the dining room with a game of

solitaire by candlelight. She let her hair down and slipped off her shoes; the wool felt good on her sore feet.

"How are you doing, baby?" Dal asked, walking in from the hall leading to the garage.

"Oh, I am all right."

"You want me to get you some coffee?"

"That would be nice."

He went to the candlelit kitchen. Teddy entered and sat down next to her.

"Generator's fried," Teddy said. "The damn thing is screwed up! It's going to be a long stuffy night cooped up in here." He paused. "Dally, pour me a Pyrat, will you?" he said, directing his voice through to the kitchen.

"Sure."

In a minute, Dal came back in with the rum and coffee, handed them to Teddy and Charlotte and sat down.

"Thanks—hey, maybe Eliza will uproot more of our ship," Teddy said.

"I was thinking the same thing. This could be a good thing."

"I like your optimism," said Teddy, holding up his glass in toast. "Cheers!" Their glasses clanged.

"Did you hear gold broke a record today - $1725?" Dal asked.

"Oh yeah, we're in the right business, that's for sure," Teddy said.

"Why is gold so popular now, anyway? Sounds like fear to me," Charlotte said.

"A lack of faith in the dollar," Teddy said.

"Why don't people trust the dollar? I just don't understand," Charlotte said, flipping her cards over and moving them around.

"You see, everything changed when President Nixon

took us off the gold standard. Ever since then, nothing has backed the dollar. When the government needs money, it turns the printers on at the Federal Reserve and writes IOUs to other nations and itself. It's like if we would go over to our computer and print money off the Hewlett Packard when our bank accounts get low. That process floods the market with an empty currency, creating inflation and an increased deficit."

"What's the silly debt now?" Charlotte asked.

"Over twenty two trillion and counting, and China owns a lot of it. And they're getting tired of financing our debt," Dal said.

"I didn't know it was that bad," Charlotte said. "So, what do you think is going to happen?"

"Well, the US Dollar is the reserve currency for the whole world. As long as other countries finance our debt by buying and holding the dollar, then we're fine. But, if they decide to dump it, and buy gold and cryptocurrency, the dollar will decline, and, well ... you get the idea."

"Well, let's pray to God that doesn't happen," Charlotte said.

"Amen to that," Teddy said.

"Amen," Dal said.

"So, what's the solution?" asked Charlotte.

Teddy looked squarely at her with an air of seriousness and said, "The solution is for our country to *really* reduce its debt, get a hold on the Federal Reserve's currency manipulation, and return to a sounder currency like a crypto that is backed by gold. Then, the faith in the dollar will be strong. Here's to financial stability for the world," Teddy said, holding up his glass and inviting another toast. They clanged their glasses with his; Dal and Charlotte made eyes; Teddy caught it.

"You two look good together."

"Thanks, Teddy. What about you? When are you going to start dating again? Cosby will be gone soon and it's going to get lonely with just you and Colt," Dal said.

"Oh, I reckon I'll do fine. I got the animals here. I don't get lonely, anyway," Teddy remarked.

"Everyone gets lonely. I see you sometimes playing chess with yourself late at night," Charlotte said, watching Teddy.

"How do you play chess alone?" Dal asked.

"It's easy, you just move for yourself and the other person," answered Teddy.

"Oh, that's really sad, Salt," Dal said, laughing.

Teddy smiled, "But I had a dream about a woman last night."

"Really? Who?" Charlotte asked.

"I don't know. It was in another time. In Spain."

Charlotte shook her head, "Teddy, dreams are wonderful, but you can't hold them, depend on them, or share a family with them. I think you should go on some dates."

"No way."

"Yeah, you should, Salt. Charlotte set Ty up with a real nice woman and it worked out—intelligent, and a looker too."

"*Really?*"

"Yeah," Dal answered.

"Well, I am not doing it. I'll find my lady one day," he barked, crossing his arms in defiance.

"You still haven't let go of Sarah, have you? I can see it in your eyes. You're waiting for her as if she could somehow come back, but she can't. You have to move on. You may find that treasure out at sea, but you won't find love. I think you should visit the graveyard," Charlotte said.

"No," remarked Teddy.

"But you have to, Teddy, it's the only thing that'll make it real for you," pleaded Charlotte.

"I am *never* going *there*." His mouth turned up as he squirmed in his chair.

"I'll take you sometime next week. You *have* to see her grave."

"Dammit Charlotte, what part of *no* don't you understand?!" He stood up and paced around the room, slicking his hair back.

"Chill out Salt, she's just trying to help. Maybe she's right, you know."

Teddy paused, looking through the glass into the indoor poolroom with his hands on his hips. "I am sorry Charlotte, I just don't like graveyards. You pushed me," Teddy said with a soft voice.

"I am sorry, Teddy. Listen, I have a real nice friend who's a chef downtown. I think you two would make a great pair." Teddy loosened up, walked back over and sat down.

"Oh come on Charlotte, no blind dates please." He gulped the Pyrat.

"Why not? I've already told her about you, and she wants to meet you. She said you sounded real interesting, with the treasure hunting and the cat sidekick."

"*Seriously* Charlotte, why'd you have to do that?

"She's beautiful and an incredible cook. She's very nice and *besides* with all that good fish you bring in, she would always have food and you would always have a cook."

He paused for a moment, tempted by the possibility of a live-in professional chef. "I do love to eat. Just how good of a cook is she?"

"She's pretty *damn* good." Dal said, "She runs that new restaurant, Blonde, downtown."

"Haven't been there, but I like the name, I guess."

"If she can play chess, you'll have it made." Dal joked.

"Come on, Teddy," Charlotte begged.

"I'll *think* about it."

"That's a yes!" Charlotte said, smiling.

"No, that's a *maybe*."

"Come on, at least check her out first, why don't you," Charlotte insisted, showing him her facebook photo on her smartphone.

"She's very pretty Charlotte, but she's not serious enough for me. I am a serious guy you know," Teddy said. "I can tell by looking at her, she's not a big thinker."

IN THE OTHER ROOM, the younger crowd chatted.

"I think we should go to California and find that damn treasure," Cos said. "It could pay my way through college, and I could pay the high school back for the cow prank."

"I want to go! I could pay for Stanford."

"Me too!" Leslie said. "Maybe I could buy a new arm. They have these sweet robotic arms now."

"Oh babe, that sounds kind of sexy," Cos said.

"You two are silly," Belle said.

"I could pay for graduate school," Joey added, his head resting in Belle's lap as she combed his wheat-colored locks with her hand.

"I would buy a brand-new Toyota Tacoma and retire the chicken mobile," Cos added.

"But I *love* the chicken!" Leslie said.

"Really?" Cos said.

"Yeah!"

"Well, maybe I could buy it from Dan, but I am quitting the fryer for sure."

"That's bull! You're never going to stand up to Dan. He would go ape shit on you," Joey said.

"Just you wait and see, bro."

"I would give it all away after paying for school of course," Belle said.

"I would too, but hopefully there would be enough left over for a new arm and a Louis Vuitton handbag," Leslie said.

"I know, I like the Tivoli GM."

"Oh, I know the one you're talking about—with the crossed leather clasps."

"Yeah, that's it."

"I like the one that has the cream-colored leather across the top going up the handles. I forget the name, but it looks like a bowtie," Leslie said.

"Oh I know that one too, I think it's even called the Bowtie PM or something like that."

"Is it really? That's funny; it's *so* cute."

"Okay, okay. Everyone just settle down. We'll all get our share of the treasure that *we don't have*," Joey said.

"There's nothing wrong with dreaming, Joey," Belle said, looking sharply down at him.

"I guess you're right."

"Dreams are what make life worth living," Belle reiterated.

"You're so right, Belleaboo. In that case, I am getting a boat."

8

Hours passed with dreams of wealth distracting everyone from the harsh winds and destruction outside the safety of Isabella's walls. A crash occurred outside and Teddy zipped into the kitchen from the dining room to see the farm drowning in water.

He shuffled back into the other room with a look of hysteria.

"What's wrong?" Dal asked.

"A storm surge has flooded the yard!"

"Oh, man," Dal said.

"Charlotte, please gather some food and take it upstairs to the library. We need to prepare in case the water keeps rising," Teddy said.

"Okay, I will get on it," she said.

"Help me put up the animals, Dal!" Teddy ordered.

"You want to go out in this weather?! Are you crazy?" Dal asked.

"No, I don't want to, I need to."

"Well you know I am your wingman, crazy or not."

Charlotte kissed Dal and straightened his collar, asking

him to be careful, then exited into the kitchen to place the food into a trunk.

Teddy and Dal strapped on waders and slickers, then Teddy grabbed a very long coiled rope from the garage.

When they went outside, fierce winds blew their bodies back and tossed water against the third step, splashing it up at their legs. Rainwater stung their eyes; reminding Teddy of being on *La Gracia*. Through the sheets of rain, he saw Joey's Chevy and his own Ford truck submerged in water, a large oak limb planted in the Chevy's front windshield. Teddy threw Dal a headlamp and tied the rope to one of the stone lions' heads at the top of the front steps, then knotted it around his waist, and then to Dal's. They waded out into the warm violence as waves bashed against their torsos, sideways rain pelleting their faces.

When they reached the tree house about thirty feet from the barn, the wind picked up and Teddy slipped and fell into the water; the current carried him away from the barn. Dal grabbed onto the ladder of the tree house and dug his waders deep into the softened ground, then he pulled on the rope one arm at a time until he reeled Teddy back to the tree. Teddy hugged him and they pushed on to the barn.

It was dark and wet inside, and the horses were loud and wild-eyed.

Taking off the rope, they looped it around a wooden stall post in the barn and treaded through the water that seeped in under the crack of the door like a bad spirit. Teddy led Caramel over to the ramp he'd constructed in case this very scenario ever happened and, with Dal's help, took her up. As they led the Arabian, Earful, up next, their muscles started to fatigue, their faces turned red, and their foreheads dripped with sweat, but they continued until all the horses were upstairs. Finally, they led Five Alarm up. After retying the ropes, they waded outside back toward the house. No way they could shepherd the chicken flock up the ramp, so they let them be.

Thirty feet from the house, the speed of the wind increased and so did the current, which knocked Teddy sideways; his weight pulled Dal with him. The current took them away from the house until the slack of the rope drew tight on the lion's head, holding them steady. Twigs and debris floated into and around them. From the water, they both grabbed hold of the rope and dug their feet into the ground; using it like a lifeline, they followed it with their hands, but the rope started to give and they fell back down. The rope held them in place, but as they pulled on it, the loose knot started to unravel from the stone lion's mane.

"*What are we going to do?*" Teddy yelled through the rain.

"I don't know!" Dal yelled back, holding on tight. Teddy considered the scenario of the knot coming undone; the current would carry them onto the back thirty acres where Eliza would tear them to shreds when she arrived. Flashes of *La Gracia* came in and out of his mind. The color of the sky was that same haunting shade and the angle of the rain exactly the same, but this time Admiral Garcia wasn't there to wind his watch for good luck and there was no boat waiting to take him to shore. The line slipped and they slid back five feet. Then, the rope caught and jiggled a little. Teddy glanced up at the front door, blocking the rain with his hand. Through the falling water, he saw Dog tugging the rope tight around the lion.

"Look Dal! Look!" Teddy said. Dal saw Dog. "Good boy! He must have come out through the cat flap," Teddy yelled through the rain.

"Good dog!" Dal yelled.

They stood back up against the force of the weather.

When they jerked again, the rope was tight so they were able to make their way to the front door. Teddy picked up Dog and kissed his head. Dog smiled. "Even though Dog loves water, he has an intense fear of storms, too. The Jack Russell is a genius, though. I swear he knew we needed his help."

After entering Isabella, they collapsed in the candlelit entryway, resting their backs against the thick mahogany door. Dal rubbed Teddy's shoulder and told him they did it. Charlotte greeted them with towels and water. After drying off, they stumbled into the living room, Dog following, and flopped into chairs.

"Boy, you may not be the best fish I've reeled in, but you sure were the hardest," Dal joked to Teddy. Teddy laughed.

"That dog saved us," Dal exclaimed to the room.

"Sure did."

The group was amazed when they explained what Dog had done.

After half an hour, Eliza's first wall arrived. Isabella shook from her pressure, like an army rushing a castle. Charlotte, Dal, and Teddy rose to go to the kitchen. A boom shook the wall to the right of the mantel. A huge oak tree branch fired through a boarded up window, sending shattered glass into the room.

"Get down!" Teddy hollered. The end pierced Ole Sawtooth's hide on the wall, just missing Dal, who reacted quickly and dived to push Teddy and Charlotte out of the way. The gust coming in knocked out some of the candles, and the picture of Luke fell, crashing on the floor.

Water leaked in through the broken boarded up window while the rain rattled on the ceramic roof. Eliza thundered into Isabella through the opening like a lion roaring that never stopped to breathe. A heavy limb from the Oak branch landed on Dal's leg and he lay on the floor in pain. Teddy saw that the limb was in the same spot as the cannon in his dream; he lifted it off and helped Dal over to a chair with Dog behind him. The ladies and young men watched from the sofas, clinging to each other.

Blood seeped from the wound. Teddy went into the kitchen to get gauze pads from a storage cabinet, cold bottled water from the fridge, and a pan to wash the water into. While he was leaving the kitchen, the impact-resistant glass exploded and a piece of wood debris flew into a glass cabinet, splattering glass everywhere. Teddy kneeled and hustled into the living room.

"What just happened?" Joey asked.

"Some flying debris broke the bay window!" answered Teddy.

"Not very resistant."

"Not to a hundred mile an hour flying piece of wood. Y'all might want to stay out of the kitchen."

He poured the Perrier on the wound and Dal grimaced in pain when the cold touched his ripped skin. Teddy nodded toward his remaining brandy on the coffee table; Dal picked it up and swallowed it in one sip. Teddy wrapped his leg with the gauze and then rested in the chair beside him, assuring the group they would be safe— his confidence was contagious, and the room relaxed with him.

After about twenty minutes, the storm slowed down and everyone breathed easier.

In a bit, they heard a screeching sound accompanied by loud thuds on the boarded windows coming from the back porch.

"What's next?" Dal asked with sweat beading on his brow.

"I don't know," Teddy said. The screeching happened again. "I'll go check it out when the eye hits."

After five minutes, the winds and rain ceased. The pounding and screeching continued, amplified now by the silence.

Picking up his Browning Safari rifle from the firearm case, Teddy walked into the calm silence on the stone back porch. Water buried the pool; debris from the pool house floated all over the yard.

What he saw next stunned him. Occupying much of the width of the back porch was a white and brown spotted hog, banging its head on the wood covering of one of the living room windows and squealing.

Teddy trotted back inside and got the rope, cut it with his CRKT pocketknife, and knotted it, making a fat loop on one end. Then, he slowly approached the hog with the rifle in one hand and the rope in the other. He wanted to lead it away from the wall before shooting it.

As it turned, they made eye contact. Teddy saw a kindness there; the hog was quiet for a moment, but just as Teddy approached, it resumed banging its head and crying. Teddy backed off with the gun, which now shook in his hand. He knew that if the hog decided to attack, it could kill him—yet, he didn't *sense* danger. Waiting for a moment, he approached a second time and managed to loop the rope around the hog's neck. While tightening it, the hog turned, staring at him. He led it away from the wall; the hog resisted at first, but to his surprise, came with ease at the second tug. After getting him out to the center of the porch, Teddy prepared to fire, but the hog just stood there, looking at him. He had hunted and killed wild hogs before, but there was something deep in this one's eyes that wouldn't let him pull the trigger, something almost beautiful ... wise. Lowering the gun, he led the hog inside to the poolroom.

"You stupid hog, you see what you're making me do? This is so stupid."

Inside, he looked at the hog, and it smiled. "Do you know you have a twenty-five-thousand-dollar reward on your head?"

The group sat in the door to the poolroom, expressing genuine bafflement at the sight of the soaking wet mammoth beast, which stood there like stone. They watched it and it watched them; it smiled and they laughed; Bear and Dog sniffed it and it wiggled its caboose at them. Teddy held the gun on it while each person entered slowly and petted him. He rubbed the side of his smiling head against Belle's knee, gazing up at her.

"Is *that* Half Ton?" Joey asked.

"I reckon it is," Teddy said.

"I can't believe he survived out there," Cos said.

"No wonder Belle's dad wants him dead; he's a beast." Joey said.

"Have you ever seen a wild hog act like this?" Teddy asked Dal.

"Well, I've never seen one that big, period. He's enormous! I haven't seen that many, but *I know this isn't right*. He's acting like a damn housecat."

"Good Lord!" Teddy said. "What are we going to do with him? He'll die if we put him back outside."

"Then let him die; he's too dangerous to keep inside," Dal said.

"I know you're right, but I can't. There's something in his eyes," Teddy said. "Is there *anywhere* we could place him?"

"*Something in his eyes?* There's something in his weight

and size too. He could kill someone, Salt, and tear this house to shreds," said Dal.

"I know, but I am keeping him."

"Well if you're going to be stupid, you might as well be smart stupid, so how about the garage?" Dal offered.

"It's flooded by now," Teddy remarked. Dal shrugged.

"What about the sauna?" Charlotte suggested.

"Yeah, that's just what the hog needs, Charlotte: a big bath," remarked Dal.

"I am just trying to be helpful." She shot him a glance.

"It's a good idea, Charlotte," Teddy said, and then led the hog down the hall to the tiled sauna. Half Ton's eyes thanked him when he closed the door. As Teddy walked away, Bear pawed at the door, meowing. Teddy returned to the living room where he patched the window around the tree with plastic, which he duct-taped in place. Then, he did the same to the kitchen window.

Teddy directed the young folks to the upstairs library for the second wall of the storm; Charlotte gave them the trunk of food, candles, and flashlights to carry up.

9

J oey led them up the ceramic stairs and down the long, tiled hall to the library at the end; Cos and Leslie carried the blankets and pillows. They entered the library, which smelled like oiled wood and old books. Ascending bookcases lined three walls, filled with knowledge on every subject. The ceiling stretched for thirty feet and an iron spiral staircase spun up to an open second level that traced each wall of books around a wooden overhang.

A desk cut from one piece of staggering oak jutted out from the front wall; animal skins from safaris and hunts covered the floors. On the wall, a coat of arms from Ireland represented the Dollarhide ancestry along with antique landscapes, deer antlers, and horns from bighorn sheep.

After scanning the majestic room, Leslie and Belle spread out pallets on the floor so the room resembled a Turkish veranda.

Leslie proceeded to light beeswax candles around the room; the rays bounced off the wood-paneled walls as the aroma of the wax filled the air. She and Belle walked around with flashlights, looking at the books.

"Y'all wanna see something sweet?" Joey asked.

"Yeah," they replied.

"Follow me."

He picked up a lit votive candle and walked over to an area of the bookcase where he removed a large dictionary. Sticking his hand in the empty space, he turned and pulled a small mechanism in the lower section of the bookcase, revealing a passage just big enough for a person to crawl through.

"What's this for?" Belle asked.

"It was built as a sort of safe room from potential robbers and as way to escape fires that might block the door," answered Joey.

"Where does it go?" Leslie asked.

"It travels around to the different guest rooms on this side of the second floor each of which have a secret door through the closets, and there's a thin ladder that leads to the third-floor tower."

"Sweeeet," Leslie remarked.

Joey placed the candle down, and pulled a flashlight from his pocket, and shone it into the space before crawling through the interior wall space. They passed a fake return air grille that allowed them to see out into the room. Leslie kept tickling Cos from behind. Finally, they made it to a guest room, exiting through a tiny door in the closet behind fur coats with the faint aroma of expensive perfume from years ago, when they went to important places.

"That was so neat," Belle said.

They walked through the stately guest room and back to the library.

Belle picked out a book of Keats and flopped down on a

quilt next to Joey. Leslie and Cos scanned the shelves until they came to a framed photo of a man with a bushy red moustache, suspenders, and a dirt-stained Henley; he wore a beat-up cowboy hat and rested on one knee. The photo's edges were faded and worn. Beside it were a series of small ancient journals. Cos dug his thumbs into Leslie's shoulders from behind; she tilted her head back and purred. He stopped and wrapped his arms around her waist, resting his chin on her shoulder.

"Is that Luke?" she asked.

"Yep, that's Luke all right."

"He looks like a real outdoorsman. What are these books?"

"Probably his journals from the gold mining days. You're welcome to take a look, but I think his penmanship is almost illegible."

"My mother's handwriting is so terrible that I can read anything."

She placed the butt of the metal flashlight in her thick lips and opened one of the books with her good arm. Cos kissed her neck. Her eyes smiled as she kept looking. He walked his mouth up toward her ear, kissing her again and again. Cos took the flashlight, and held it for her, looking over her shoulder. She skimmed through the age-dyed pages of pencil sketches of the Sierras. A beaver filled one page, various birds adorned others, and on another was a grizzly bear.

"Oh, that must be Ole Saw!" she said, pointing to the bear.

"Must be! Ole Saw! Ha!"

"What an artist."

"Yeah, Luke was very talented. He did a lot of the framed animal drawings in our house."

"I am going to look through this some more. Maybe we can find a clue as to where the treasure is buried." She took the books to the pallets and he went with her.

The second wall of the storm arrived, shaking the house like a drum. They took comfort in the softness of the quilts and the warmth of each other. Joey wrapped his legs around Belle's thighs, drawing her to him while she read. Cos held Leslie around the waist as she flipped through the journals.

"Look right here, in this drawing, there's a river and a point sticking out from the mountain marked with a black circle. Perhaps that was the location of the treasure?"

"Might be," Cos remarked, taking the book from her hands and looking at it. "Interesting, I wonder if Teddy has seen this. It says 'see p. 22 in journal no. 4 for aerial map.'" He jumped up to look at the other journals on the bookshelf, but none of their spines was numbered 4. It was missing. Leslie picked up another journal, which was almost a complete diary. Skimming through it, she skipped over the banal daily routines about Sam and the progress in the mine—but toward the end, a page of chicken scratch caught her attention.

"Y'all listen, listen!" The room became silent as she read aloud.

"Yesterday Sam and I got thrown in jail in Bagby after a drunken cheat started a bar fight with us at the Bearfoot Saloon because we cleaned up at poker. While in jail, the sheriff brought in a distraught Indian fellow who had been stabbed in the stomach by a white soldier who was part of a cavalry that attacked his people. In the middle of the night, he woke me, explaining that he would be sentenced to execution the next day, claimed he knew the location of a certain treasure by John Hodges's gang; his tribe had stolen and buried it. Said it was in the High Sierras at the foot of a mountain where the rock comes out toward the south side of the river so close to the edge that the traveler has to hug the water to pass the base of it. He insisted it would be back up the path roughly ten feet. He made me promise to deliver half of the gold to his people if I found it, and the other half, I could keep.

Some entries later, the journal read:

Sure enough, we found the place and dug there for two weeks, but never found the gold. We left assuming the man was either mad or mistaken about the spot."

Leslie's eyes grew big as saucers and she shook Cos.

"*Look! That's it! That's it! Look!* I was right about the drawing, that's where they searched for the treasure and thought it was but couldn't find it."

"That's unbelievable!" Belle said after Leslie finished.

"That's amazing," Joey said. "Let me see it, please." She tossed the black book to him and he read it to himself. "I don't think Dad has given these journal entries much attention. This data is like a good dog, it hunts!"

"He's always been too busy with *La Gracia*," remarked Cos. "I am only making like minimum wage at Dan's. Anyone wanna go to California?"

"Me!" Leslie said.

"Me too!" Belle added.

Joey remarked, "I don't know y'all, maybe Teddy is right. It could take weeks or months to find it. If it even exists."

"But we know it exists! We have the evidence right here," Cos said.

"But what if we go all that way and don't find anything? Old boy Luke didn't find it," Joey said.

"Why don't we just make it a road trip? We could see Jimmy and Bo on the way and then end at Camp Big Bear, which is in the area. I am sure our old camp counselor,

Aspen, would lend us a cabin. We could play slaughter ball and capture the flag. *Then*, go look for it," Cos said.

"That could work," Joey

"Did you say *Camp Big Bear*?" Belle said, leaning up.

"Yeah, why?" Joey asked.

"I went to *Arrowhead*!"

"No way! Cos and I went to Big Bear, the brother camp. The area in the Sierras where Luke's mine was located is next to them, that's how Dad found out about Big Bear."

"I can't believe this," Belle exclaimed.

"Why did your parents send you all the way out there?" Joey asked.

"Dad wanted me to learn to shoot guns, ride horses, and bow hunt. Arrowhead was the only place."

"I didn't go to either, but I love road trips, capture the flag, and bow hunting," Leslie said.

"What do y'all say?" Cos asked.

"We'll think about it," Joey said.

"Well Leslie and I are going, with or without y'all," Cos remarked.

The pounding of the storm returned, the wind howled; they heard a slam outside and assumed another tree got struck—they waited for the impact, but it timbered in the yard. Soon enough, they stopped talking and lay close to each other; after a while, Cos got up to blow out the candles, sending them into darkness.

As Joey held Belle, he could feel her erratic tension. Thinking he might be too close, he asked her what was wrong. She whispered in his ear that she was very afraid of the dark and usually slept with a light on. He leaned over and sparked a candle in a glass votive; she thanked him and relaxed.

He rolled over and stared up at the distant ceiling. He

placed his hands behind his head and Belle laid her head on his chest; her red hair felt like silk under his chin. She rubbed his arm with the tip of her fingernail.

"What are you thinking about Joey?" she said, looking at up at him with her big blue saucers, the left still dimmer than the right but just as electric.

"I am thinking that maybe we could go for it."

"I want to go."

"We'll think about it okay?" Joey said.

"*Okay.*"

THE SECOND WALL passed and the storm slowed down as it blew inland.

Teddy and the adults had decided to stay downstairs to monitor the potential flooding and only move upstairs if the waters rose high enough. He knocked on the library door and the couples moved away from each other as he entered. Now that the storm was gone, he insisted the ladies stay in the guest rooms. Joey and Cos' rooms were respectively downstairs anyway. "If I hear one door close from downstairs, I am coming up with Bear to sic him on some toes."

Joey and Cos laughed. The ladies agreed and exited. Teddy closed the door behind them.

Joey waited a few minutes, then rose and walked out the door.

"Hey, what did I say?" Teddy said as he leaned to the side of the hall wall where he was waiting.

"Sorry Dad, but I am a man now. I just want to talk to her."

"Talk? Yeah, sure. It's late, son."

"All right Dad—goodnight." Joey slinked back into the

library. After ten minutes, he took the flashlight and crept through the passage in the wall, sneaking to Belle's room. As he rounded the corner, the light shone on Belle heading toward him in an oversized T-shirt and underwear and they both started to laugh.

When they reached each other, he set the light down, cupped her neck in his hand, and they kissed while still on their knees.

"I just couldn't stand being away from you any longer," he whispered in between breaths.

"I know. I just want to be alone with you so bad."

She sucked his lip and he softly bit hers. She pushed him back to the floor and fell forward on top of him. Leaning up, she slightly bumped her head on the low ceiling and they both laughed. They kissed and kissed for a long time and then he touched her under her shirt. Then, he glided the edge of one of his fingernails along her waist-line and she grinned but stopped him, then whispered in his ear that she had to leave—the push of her breath warm against his skin. He begged her to stay, but she insisted, and by the light of the flashlight, she crawled away, leaving him twisted and tangled, crazy and thirsty. He went back to the library. They both fell asleep that night with visions of the other amid long forgotten memories of summers in the Sierras streaming through their minds like rapids in the river there.

Downstairs, Teddy slept in his room while Dal slept on one of the living room couches, resting his bandaged leg on the ottoman with Charlotte by his side. The butterflies were at peace in the aquarium, and the house was still.

10

Teddy opened the front door while carrying the butterfly aquarium; Dal limped out behind him. The water had receded in the night—plants, limbs, and trees covered the land, the June sun illuminating it in a surreal haze of humidity and heat. The rosebushes under the kitchen window lay beaten to pieces. A tree lay across the driveway, and the oak limb still sat on top of Joey's waterlogged Chevy. A twister had ripped *Uncle Benny* off the tree house and slung it up the driveway where it rested, broken in two.

Teddy walked onto the grass, set the aquarium down, and opened it. With some encouragement, the swallowtails burst into the white sunlight; he and Dal watched them as they dispersed.

Walking over to the barn, he checked on the horses and the bull; they all seemed to be okay. He led each one of them down. His heart swelled with gratitude. After petting the horses, he let them out to graze. Next, he walked toward Windswept Street. Three short trees blocked the road, and leaf and limb debris littered the sand-dusted asphalt.

Returning to the house, Dal and he gazed out over the mess in silent disbelief. After surveying the land, Teddy gathered parts from the Dog House and repaired the generator and converter over the next hour. The power kicked on and Isabella breathed again. Then, he removed the plywood covering her windows so she could see.

He emailed his buddy Sam Boxfly with the Coast Guard for an update via his smartphone.

Back inside, Teddy got the rope leash and checked on Half Ton. The hog rose, lowering his head so Teddy could leash him. The act amazed Teddy. He guided the hog out the kitchen door, which Ton could just squeeze through. Then, he placed him in the horse ring to the right of the barn.

Next, Teddy woke the younger folks, leaving some clothes Charlotte gave him for the ladies at the door. Dog came in from downstairs and licked Cos's face; Cos pushed him off. The girls and guys took turns showering.

Belle bumped into Joey in the hall after getting out, dressed in an oversized Florida Marlins t-shirt, her wet hair tossed over one shoulder. He shook his head with a grin, checking her out. She smiled and pushed him lightly as they walked by—he tried to kiss her, but she dodged it, teasing him.

"This water is like bathing in a mountain stream. I love it," she said to him.

"It's well water, so it feels that way."

"That explains it. My hair loves it," she said, walking to the room to change.

The men threw on canvas shorts, T-shirts, and shoes, and Joey grabbed the two journals. Then, they went outside to survey the damage.

Teddy was back outside, standing shirtless on the hood

of the Chevy, chain-sawing the limb into pieces. He idled the saw for a minute, glancing up over his gold Ray Bans.

"Your Chevy got ruined by the storm, Joey."

The group stood stupefied by the mass of fallen trees and *Uncle Benny*. Belle started crying, then buried her face in Joey's shirt; he stood there speechless.

"God, I hope my parents are all right," Belle said. She and Leslie took out their phones, but still couldn't get a signal.

Joey comforted Belle.

After a while, Joey and Belle headed off to inspect the tree house. Climbing the stairs, they dodged two broken steps. Leaves and twigs carpeted the deck like autumn in Connecticut. His hammock still hung from two posts like a weathered victory flag. They walked in through the front door to the left of the four-foot-wide trunk. The inside was a tile floor with painted white wood walls and ceilings. A mini-refrigerator sat in the entrance next to a stainless steel sink; an antique French baker's table facing the screened window served as a desk. The oak's trunk made the right wall, which curved through the space, and a signed picture of Ted Williams hung crooked from a nail in the fat bark. Cut holes in the floor allowed two big limbs to whip through the room; about an inch of water covered the floor.

"Wow Joey, I love this! It's like you're outside, but you're inside. Did Teddy build this for you?"

"Thanks! No, I built it, but Dad designed it and got me started."

He gave her the tour, taking her up a spinning staircase to a loft. Exiting onto a small porch, he pried off the board covering the screen, revealing a peek-a-boo view of the blue ocean over the small trees and houses in the distance. Some of the houses had trees on top of them, and many of the oceanfront properties were damaged or destroyed.

"What a view!" she exclaimed.

Standing there with his hands on his hips, he took a deep breath. "Yep, this is my sweet spot. It's where I used to come to get away or clear my head before a game. When it rains, you can hear it on the tin roof."

"I love the sound of rain on a tin roof. It's heaven," Belle paused. "It looks like very little damage occurred."

"This oak is pretty strong. Unfortunately, *Uncle Benny* got blown off." He looked down on the yard at it. "I'll have to replace him with something else. I'll probably just build an extension there."

Reluctantly drinking in the devastation, Belle placed her hand to her mouth and cried. Joey leaned in and held her.

"Don't cry baby, I am sure your parents are fine."

"I know, but what about Latch, it's just *so* sad."

He took her delicate hand and kissed it.

"It'll be all right, I promise. At least we're together."

After holding each other, some of their sadness drained away. In a minute, they joined the rest of the group. They stood around the horse ring, laughing at Half Ton. Colt threw one of Dog's rubber toys and the fat hog retrieved it with a smirk on his face, his tail slightly wiggling. Bear sat on the wooden fence watching his new friend in approval. Three swallowtail butterflies from the chimney perched on the fence. They flew off occasionally only to return shortly after.

"I swear this hog is domesticated," Teddy said. His phone beeped with an incoming email from Boxfly:

Glad y'all are okay. She was a strong Cat 2. Town is a mess. Windows broken, power out, electric lines and trees blocking intersections, trees on homes, people fighting at gas stations. The surge made landfall five miles south of Latch, badly flooding the Ball neighborhood and an old people's home. Stay home and if you come out, be careful! Box

Teddy knew the report would be bad, but he didn't know *how* bad. He walked over to the yard and relayed a summary of Box's message to the group, insisting that Cos and Joey walk the girls home because they couldn't drive.

"Are we keeping Half Ton?" Cos asked.

"I guess so," Teddy said, looking at the hog. "He seems to like it here, and we like him. Bear certainly does."

"Good, I like the big fellow," Cos said.

"I won't tell my father about him, it'll be our little secret. I don't know why he cares so much anyway."

"Thank you, Annabelle. Normally, I wouldn't care, but there's something about the hog's eyes, you know."

"I think I know what you mean. I see it, too."

Breakfast wafted out the open kitchen window, stirring their stomachs.

"Why don't y'all go eat. It'll set your minds at ease." Heeding his advice, they wandered inside; Teddy caught Joey.

"Jojo, wait a minute." Joey stopped and backtracked.

"Before you take Belle and Leslie home, go into my office and get the Glock, just to be safe. I don't want one of those gasoline-siphoning weirdos to hurt you."

"Sure thing." Joey started to walk off, but stopped. "Oh, I almost forgot. I have to show you something, Dad." He opened the first black journal he had in his hand to the dog-eared drawing of the mountain before handing it to Teddy. Teddy studied it, and then Joey passed him the second one, pointing to the entry describing Luke's meeting with the

Native American. In disbelief, Teddy placed his hand on Joey's shoulder.

"You know, I thumbed through some of these when we inherited Isabella and all Red's possessions, but I didn't see this. You could build a hunt around this. Are you thinking about it?"

"Yeah, maybe. Cos owes the school a lot of money, and I would like to go to graduate school at some point without taking out a loan."

"Good."

"We're missing journal number four, though. Any idea where it is?" Joey asked.

"Your uncle Bo in Santa Fe took some of Red's possessions; I bet he has it."

"Great! We could go see him on the way to California," Joey said.

"Y'all have my best if you go. Just be careful." Teddy handed Joey the journals. Looking at Teddy, he saw himself smiling back in the mirrored aviators.

"Thanks, Dad."

"You're welcome, Son."

Joey pranced inside high off Teddy's encouragement and removed the Glock from the firearm case. He took out a box of bullets, loaded the pistol, and slipped it into the back waistline of his canvas duck shorts with the safety on. He threw the box away, but it missed the trashcan, skipping behind the desk. Reaching for it, he felt a paper airplane back there. Unfolding it, he read Isabella's notice of seizure if taxes weren't paid. His eyebrows pointed up; his mouth frowning.

Dal rested at the bamboo dining table with his bandaged leg propped up on a chair. Charlotte waltzed around him whistling, opening windows to let light and fresh air in. Then, she set the table with homemade jams mixed with whole fruit and honey, fresh butter, a bowl of fresh cherries, blueberry pancakes, a pitcher of freshly squeezed orange juice, and a platter of scrambled eggs. Dog was trailing her legs for a hand out. Joey entered, shook up.

Outside, Teddy got a text from Bob Barclay offering same-day tree service to his clients. Unlike the girls who had a different cell service provider, Teddy could receive text messages, but *still* could not make any calls. Teddy texted him fast to get in first; Bob responded immediately, prefacing with, "I told you it would be big."

The group ate. After finishing, they went outside and said goodbye to Teddy, who had started building a pen for Half Ton. Then, they made their way out the long driveway, down Windswept and onto Orange, and out to Route 1, climbing over fallen trees that lay like dead soldiers along the road. Dog led, sniffing the ground.

The hurricane-code houses along the oceanfront did well, while those built before the storm codes had been enacted looked like a pile of broken popsicle sticks. Demolished mailboxes slept in the grass; a fractured Chevron sign hung sideways at the station; waterlogged cars melted in the heat with their windshields cracked or blown out. The scene saddened the group.

Leslie lived in downtown, and Belle two streets off Route 1 near the bay, so the group split at the edge of town.

Joey and Belle crept along the empty park. Dead fish lifted from their natural habitat by the surge lay in the green grass, which glowed healthfully in the sun. The flowerbeds lay broken and the petals on the roses around the fountain were gone, only the thorns and empty vines remaining.

Cutting down a street, they turned onto the Burns's street and arrived at the house, dodging a limb in the driveway. The house—a two-story red brick affair, unusual for a Floridian bay home—was weathered, but high enough on an incline with a raised foundation to have dodged the flooding. A midnight blue Maybach, and a dark brown Cadillac Escalade—the color, a nod to his wife's Texas alma mater—were parked in the driveway on a slight incline. Joey marveled at the Maybach. Limbs and seaweed were everywhere around the cars.

Joey tied Dog up to the front railing and they walked up the red brick steps through the opened front door. She called to her parents. The wallpaper softened the sound. The formal entry had a wooden staircase leading to upstairs. Potpourri sat on a lowboy under a Thomas Kinkade painting of an English village with a cobblestone street in winter.

Belle's mother, Patsy, a slim lady in her late forties with brown hair and a lilac top, rushed to greet them.

"We were so worried about you, honey."

"I know, I was worried about y'all too," Belle said as her mother hugged her tight. "I am so glad to see you're all right. How did y'all do?"

"Oh, we did fine. Are you all right? You're not *hurt*, are you?" Patsy studied her with a concerned look.

"We did *fine*. I am fine, Mom—*really*. Mom, this is Joey. We went to high school together. His father was nice enough to let me spend the night. Their house is unbelievable, it's this dream house with secret passages. You gotta see it sometime."

"That sounds very interesting, honey. Hello Joey, it's nice to meet you. Thank you for letting her stay," Patsy said, shaking his hand with compassionate eyes.

Belle's father, Will, a fit man with Mediterranean skin, black slicked-back hair, tortoise-rimmed Paul Smith glasses, a Patek Phillipe tank watch with a smooth crocodile band and a navy alligator golf shirt came in from the living room and hugged Belle.

"Hi Dad, Mom says everything is okay."

"Everything is fine, sweetheart. Just a few trees down. I am so glad you're all right," he said with a long Texas drawl while hugging her.

Patsy said goodbye to Joey and ushered Belle off to see Paige. While walking away, she told Joey she would call him later.

Will extended a hairy hand. Joey took it and Will squeezed his hand as if to crush the bones.

"Will Burns. Good to meet you, Joey. Nice firm hand-shake you got there. You can tell a lot about a man from his handshake."

"Yes, you can. Nice to meet you too." Will's hands were cold.

"Come into my office and take a seat." Joey agreed and followed where he took a seat facing Will's desk. Will took his place in a black Eames chair behind a French Empire desk. He removed a Cohiba Habano cigar from a box and lit it before leaning back. Joey recognized the familiar smell from his house.

"Quite a storm last night."

"Yes, sir. My father got news it was a strong Cat 2."

"That's what my secretary told me. Whew!"

"I hope everyone in town is all right."

"I do too," Will said. "How did Belle end up at your house again?"

"There was a graduation party at the beach. When it started to rain really hard, we got caught in it. Mr. Burns, I just want you to know we had no intentions of her staying at my house during the hurricane."

"I know son, I am just curious. Besides, Belle is a grown woman now. She can do as she pleases."

"Thank you for understanding."

"Of course—cigar?" Will said, extending the box to him.

"No, sir."

"Cohiba. They're the best. I only smoke the best."

"No, thank you."

Will paused, "You play baseball, don't you?" He drew on the cigar.

"I played, but got injured last year. I just graduated."

"You were pretty good, right?"

"I was all right."

"Ohhh, you're being modest, son. I heard through *The Grapevine* that you were the best high school prospect to come out of Florida in years and that you played ball in Cal-i-fornia?"

"That's what some people said before I got hurt, but the injury cooked my chances at the majors."

He puffed. "That's too bad. Belle likes Cal-i-fornia. Wants to go to Stanford Business School—she got in, too." He stood, moving to the window and looking out, while gesturing with his cigar as he spoke, "Pretty impressive feat, getting into Stanford Business School." He took another long drag off the cigar.

"Yes, Mr. Burns, I am sure you're very proud of her." Will turned around and paced.

"Yes, I am, Joey. Of course, Texas is where her sister and cousins go, and where my wife went, and her sisters and parents went. You get the picture."

Joey was quiet, shifting in his chair as Will held eye contact.

"Your father fishes professionally?"

"Yes, but he also hunts treasure."

"Treasure, *really*?"

"Yes, sir. He says that all treasure hunting *is* fishing in a way. Belle tells me you're into oil. I guess oil is kind of like fishing too."

"It's a *little* different, son," Will said with a condescending tone. "You see, I own that oil and make money each time I sell it. Drilling for oil is more like harvesting a crop than fishing. Less chance."

"Treasure hunting is not chance; it's very calculated." Joey was irritated, knowing Will was well aware of the risk in drilling oil.

"Fairytales are good things to tell children when they go to sleep at night, but they have no place in the real world."

Joey wanted to leave, but his care for Belle kept him in the seat. "I don't like people insulting my father. If you do it again, I am leaving."

"Whoa, hold on son, I am not insulting anyone, only illustrating that we're in a different business. That's all." Will plopped down again and paused, the silence uncomfortable.

"Belle tells me you have a farm?"

"Yes."

"Do you have horses?"

"Yes, three."

"You see this horse?" He pointed to a photo on the wall. "Do you know what that is?"

Joey looked at the picture.

"An Arabian, by the ears."

"Very good, you know your breeds, son."

"Yeah, well, we have one at the farm, named Earful."

"*Really?*"

"Yes."

"Well, mine is a stallion, and he lives on a farm in Kentucky. His lineage is *perfect*."

Will sucked the cigar like a straw and then blew a cloud of smoke at Joey—it hit him like a punch in the face. "Of course, they can only breed with the highest quality Arabian mare or the offspring will be tainted. It's a *pure* breed line."

"Are we talking about horses?"

"We're talking about *breeding* stallions."

"If you want to say something to me, *say* it like a man."

"I think I already have."

"Make it clearer so that I understand. Am I welcome to hang out with Belle?"

Will held eye contact and leaned forward with his elbows on his desk, punching the cigar. "Some wild horses just can't be tamed, Joey. All the treasure in the world can't make a poor quarter horse into an Arabian stallion."

"I don't have to take this from you. I may care for your daughter, but I think you're an arrogant prick." Joey got up and stormed out the door. Will smiled. "Look forward to seeing you again, Joey. Don't be shy now."

Joey slammed the front door, rushing out into the driveway. He couldn't breathe and kicked one of the bushes hard and trampled out into the street.

As he headed home, he couldn't fathom how Will and such a delicate creature like Belle were related.

Belle swung into her father's office.

"Hey Dad, what did you and Joey talk about?"

"The weather, horses, you know—man stuff."

"Well, be nice to him, I have a big crush on him."

"Really, Belle? You know he's the son of a salvager."

"He's a treasure hunter, Dad, *not* a salvager."

"Treasure, salvage, same thing. He's completely irrational. Hasn't been willing to sell that old rundown mansion or the land around it for years, even for way more than it's worth," Will said. "And he won't even wear a shirt around the yacht club. *The yacht club!* What about Lawrence? He just graduated from SMU."

"Ugh, Lawrence wears his fraternity ring to sleep at night. I like Joey, Dad. Get used to it."

"Oh jeez, I guess I'll try."

"How did the hunt for Half Ton go?" she asked, knowing the answer.

"Didn't get him, but we will, even if we have to raise the reward and get everyone in the town after him."

"What's the big deal, anyway? It's just a stupid hog."

"He's stirring things up—people are afraid, and we can't have that."

"Oh well, I am just glad to know y'all are all right from the storm. Hopefully the town will be fine," Belle said.

"Yes, I do hope so."

"I want you to know I've made up my mind to go to Stanford in the fall."

Will tried to hide the frown. "But I thought you had decided on Texas dear."

"No, *you* had decided."

"Did that Dollarhide boy put you up to this?" Will said, raising his voice.

"No, this is my decision, Dad."

"I knew he was no good. I just *knew* it. He's planting bad ideas in your head about places and things. I want you to stay away from him."

"You're not listening. This is what I want to do and I am dating Joey now, so get used to it."

Will stood and looked out the window. "You're *so stubborn* Belle, you get it from your mother. You know Texas is a better *fit* for you and our family. You'll be closer to us and your sisters."

"I am going to Stanford and this conversation is over!" She walked out as he shook his head.

Cos and Leslie arrived at her 40s bungalow in town across the street from the square. Her mother, Donna, a massage therapist and yoga teacher, sported black spandex workout pants and white On running shoes . She swung open the door with a smile, picked Leslie up, and squeezed her. She hugged Cos too, thanking him for letting Leslie stay and welcoming him in. They went into the warm living room where she brought them iced tea. The power was still out, but the sun waved in through the big rectangular windows. Leslie's father, Mike Gooch, walked in wearing tight stonewashed jeans and a "Gooch's" T-shirt with a drawing of a redfish on the front; he hugged Leslie and shook Cos's hand. He had curly black hair and a sense of gravitas. After asking about their house, they exchanged storm stories.

Mike owned an outdoor clothing store called Gooch's downtown and feared Eliza would hurt the economy, which had been weakened by a recent recession. If business lessened, he might lose the store. He explained that most people in Latch were tight-fisted with their greenbacks and refused to spend when the slightest ripple occurred in either the local or national economy; no reason to blame them, he explained—they were wise—but it distressed the retail industry there. A power pole broke the front glass at Gooch's, knocking out the display cases of sunglasses, he added. Realizing that her father would not be able to cover the tuition for her college, she decided not to mention it, and lovingly consoled him.

After some usual after-the-hurricane talk, she and Cos

walked outside; he combed her blonde hair back, held and kissed her. He suggested Gooch's might be one more reason to go for Hodge's treasure. He said they could turn the hog over to Will Burns, but Teddy would be so upset—his passion ruled his decision-making, and he loved that animal. She agreed, and he promised to call soon.

When he arrived home, Teddy and Joey were building the pigpen with scrap wood from the workshop. Cosby lent a hand, and Joey kept the incident at Belle's to himself.

THE NEXT DAY, Charlotte and Dal rested in the living room on the couch with Dal's leg propped up on the ottoman. Earlier that morning, Charlotte had re-dressed the wound. She rubbed his back and hair; he proposed they go out to Ink, a new seafood restaurant at a chic boutique hotel, as soon as his leg healed and things were better. She agreed and flowed off to get them coffee. When she came back in, Dal studied her face. She was forty-eight years old and beautiful, like a Renaissance statue of a princess. When she was younger, she traveled the world as a model and had lived in Paris where she married a famous photographer— he left her for a younger woman shortly after, so she returned to her hometown of Latch. Afraid her beauty had kept her from true love by attracting a shallow mate, she retreated from it—hadn't worn make up or let her hair down in ages. She even often wore fake artsy glasses to look smarter, and then there was the extra weight like a chain-mail over her figure and heart that nothing could get through. But the romance with Dal had awakened a radiance that shone from the inside, and lately she realized her beauty had always come from inside. She had always thought it was the *way she looked* that attracted people to her, but it was *who* she was that was the source of her magnetism.

Dal began to cough. After feeling his forehead, her eyebrows went up and she suggested he had an infection from the wound.

"Maybe Teddy has something, I'll go check."

"All right sweetheart," Dal said. "Hold on. I love you."

"I like you too, Dal," she said, recoiling a bit.

"I *know,* but I *love* you. Why won't you say it?"

"I don't know. I just don't like *that* word. It gives me the creeps. Besides, I care for you more than any word can convey," she said, and kissed his forehead. He frowned and let her go. She exited to the yard to get Teddy, telling him that Dal felt ill; he dropped the hammer and removed his work gloves.

"I have just the thing," he said, swinging his legs over the front of the new pen, hustling over to her with a smile. His chest and arms were soaking wet with perspiration.

"You seem awfully chipper today, considering the storm."

"I just figure, why let it upset me? So we lost some trees and have some damage. Big deal. I am more concerned about the people in Ball and the town's economy."

"I kinda see your point. So what are you going to give Dal?"

"You remember the elixir that cured Bear?"

"The wine?"

"Yes."

"Can it be used on people?"

"I've taken it."

"Is that supposed to comfort me?"

"I am still here, aren't I?"

"All right, let's do it."

They walked into Isabella and went to the living room, where Teddy placed his hand on Dal's back.

"Charlotte says you're a little under the weather?"

"A little bit. I'll be fine tomorrow."

"You look pretty sick. I have something I think will help. Will you try it?"

"I don't know. What is it?"

"Some of that wine from *La Gracia* I told you about that cured Bear. I take it anytime I get sick, and it works. Trust me."

"If you say it's safe, I trust you."

"Okay."

Teddy poured the elixir and Dal sipped it and grimaced. Rather than complain, he took it all down in the second sip.

"Whew! That's like shooting whiskey."

"It'll make your toes curl." Teddy laughed. "It just has a lil knockback, that's all. Let's see how you do with that dose. We'll give you another tonight if needed."

Teddy went outside and finished up Half Ton's pen, then led the hog into it. The boys joked about the wild hog's docility. Bear showed endless fascination with Half Ton, who reciprocated the admiration by playing with him. After about fifteen minutes of horseplay, the oddest thing happened: Bear jumped up onto the hog like an old cowboy mounting a mustang. The broad back gave him plenty of room to ride. They laughed and pointed at him. Teddy suggested Bear had found himself a horse. They laughed again and eventually wandered off to clean up the property.

After hours of backbreaking work cleaning up debris, vacuuming and shocking the pool, and vacuuming the water out of the preservation room, garage, and barn, the group was tired and sweaty. Dusk fell and the night was wet in the high eighties. They retired.

The next day, Bob showed up early at the gate, so Teddy brought Half Ton around into one of the stables in the barn, Bear following; then, he buzzed Bob in.

Bob pulled up and hopped down off the truck to greet Teddy. A Duck Masters camouflaged trucker hat hung a little off center on his head and he had a button-up white starched shirt tucked into tight Wranglers that rode below his belly, secured by a brass belt buckle in the shape of the state of Florida. Teddy greeted him, asking how he got down the road. Bob explained the city cleaned the trees up yesterday afternoon. After walking around the property, Bob counted twenty fallen trees and quoted him an enormous amount. Teddy couldn't believe it, but the work was beyond him, so he accepted. He asked Bob to please stay out of the barn because they were breaking a wild horse stabled there.

Teddy walked to the house distressed, knowing the amount would total his personal savings. He was surprised to see Dal standing up in the dining room. The color had returned to his face in one day. Every time Teddy saw the wine work, his conviction grew.

"How are you doing, Dal?"

"I am better. I think that stuff really helped me. Even my leg feels better."

"Good! It doesn't always work that fast, but I am glad it has."

"Well, I am not well, but I am better."

Outside, Joey and Cos started to build a wall out of wood where the ship ripped off the tree house.

"So you and Belle, it *finally* happened."

"Yeah, finally," Joey replied. "What about you, how's it going with Leslie?"

"Leslie is the best," Cos said. Joey grinned and shook his head.

"It's great having you home, Jojo," Cosby continued.

"Yeah, well, I am really glad to be here. I love how hot Florida gets; I could get used to this again. There is nothing like a good humid eighty-eight degrees."

"Well, we could get used to having you again." He paused. "You seem a little down since taking Belle home."

"Yeah, I met her father and he's real piece of work."

"A jerk?"

"Totally."

"I am sorry to hear it, but so what? You're not dating him."

"I don't know. She seems really close to him. It could be a problem."

"Don't bail yet, just see how it goes. Pass me the hammer."

"You're probably right." Joey handed him the hammer.

"Listen, I found out Leslie's dad's store is in trouble."

"Gooch's? No way, I love that place."

"I know, it's bad. Between that and my debt with the school, I am going for Hodge's treasure next week. Are you in?"

"Sure, I actually had already decided to go."

"Great! What changed your mind?"

"Look, I didn't want to tell you, but Dad may lose Isabella. He can't make the property tax payments, and he's so stubborn, I worry that instead of selling off some of the land, it'll be seized by the state and the whole property will be auctioned off—and we know who will be at the top of the bidding."

"*What?*" Cos stopped working, almost dropping the hammer.

"Yeah, I saw the letter in his office, folded up like an airplane."

"That's bad news. Do you think the Hodges's gold would give us enough to help?"

"I don't know, but if we could buy him even six months, he might find *La Gracia* in that time. He keeps saying how close he is."

"Okay, let's go to California then."

"Awesome. I can put some money together. Put your notice in with Dan and we'll shoot for this coming week. Don't tell Belle or Leslie until I figure things out."

"Deal." They fist bumped.

Buzz wandered into the barn looking for a restroom. He despised being on the Dollarhide farm. Every time he saw Cos walking around, the image of the surfer boy and Leslie on the beach flashed through his mind; he clenched his fists, his head became hot, pounding with anger. He loved her so much, and now this loser who couldn't even block a linebacker and had to play baseball instead of football was dating *his* girl. On the way to the can, he heard a loud snorting from inside one of the stables and peeked over. Shocked by the sheer size of Half Ton, he backpedaled a bit. Regaining his composure, he looked over again, smiling. Half Ton was so long, he almost couldn't turn around in the stable.

"Oh my God, this whopper is gonna make me rich *and* I'll get a shot at Cosby. Two for one," he whispered. He strutted out of the barn to his buddy Mike.

"Mike, you're not going to believe what I just found!"

"Your balls?" Mike said, unimpressed.

"No. Half Ton."

"*What? You found* Half Ton? *Where?*"

"In the barn; Mr. Dollarhide has him in a horse pen."

"Why would he have a feral hog in a stable?"

"Who cares! All I know is he's there and he's a damn beast. Just come look, and quit being so dense."

Buzz led and Mike followed. They sneaked into the barn and Mike glanced over into Half Ton's stall. He looked at Buzz with a smile that revealed his missing teeth, then he threw his arm around Buzz and they walked out.

THE PEARLMAKERS - BOOK 2
THE DOLLARHIDE MYSTERY

The following is an excerpt from the second book in *The Pearlmakers* trilogy. It's available now in ebook and paperback.

∼

Over the next week, FEMA came in and repaired some damage and cleaned up the town. The water in the poor, low-lying Ball neighborhood eventually receded, leaving many of the houses unrecognizable. Over twenty people died, and the survivors fled to stay with family and friends or sought temporary housing in the community center. Most were left homeless. The national news focused on an enormous neglected sewage line that broke in the Ball neighborhood, spewing into the floodwater. Many of those residents were too poor to evacuate to another town and stay in a hotel and the auditoriums were hopelessly full. Some stayed put and others swam for safer areas. Of those who swam, many got ill. The sick were being treated at the community center; some had already died.

In town, cars passed along the streets and roads as people left their shelters; logs and piles of debris still lined the roads like bad souvenirs. The power had returned, and grocery stores and a few restaurants had opened.

A couple of days after the storm, people began to see Stern Banks's black GMC Yukon with tinted windows squirming the streets like a drug dealer, stopping at destroyed or injured homes to make unapologetically low offers. Some desperate owners caved, assuming the area wouldn't recover and it might be their only chance to sell. Although the move shocked some residents, Teddy was disgusted but unsurprised.

Meanwhile, the receding surge water left an alligator stranded who had gone "land shark" downtown, snooping around people's yards at night, harassing pets, and living off raccoons and possums. Although there had been reports of seeing something that appeared large and lizard-like in the shadows of bushes at night, no one had actually seen the gator in broad daylight until Miss Jimmy spotted him smack dab in the center of the road while opening the Malt; she claimed he was as white as a ghost. She ran inside and called Officer Catfish, but by the time he arrived, the albino had vanished. A few days later, he managed to snap into her friend's running shoe and chomp on it while she screamed in terror and ran away from the beast. Knowing Teddy was well versed with amphibious things, Catfish contacted him to see if he could help track the beast and take care of it. Teddy said he would meet him in a couple of days, armed and ready.

Cleaning up the yard, making repairs to Isabella, and buying a new truck squashed Teddy's savings. With the ultimatum on the back taxes, he *had* to find something soon.

Thanks to the *La Gracia* wine, Dal's infection was gone and his leg was healed. Now, they would be ready to hunt again soon.

The Indians forfeited their regional baseball game due to the storm, which Cos had already been blackballed from playing in due to the cow prank.

Meanwhile, Belle had been texting and calling Joey. He answered by not answering. He didn't know how to tell her the truth about what her father had said to him.

To numb the pain, he turned his attention to California with Cos. They agreed to leave in the morning. Cos had given vacation notice last week to Dan, who informed him they would be closed for two weeks anyway due to Eliza.

Joey's Chevy was cooked and had a cracked windshield, so, Cos spun a story for Dan: the chicken wagon needed an oil change and new brake pads, and Teddy would fix it for free while Cos was on vacation. Baited by the word "free," Dan agreed, instructing him to bring it back when he returned. Cos called Leslie and told her they were going to California, but Leslie said she wanted to stay at home with her family due to the damage at Gooch's.

To finance the trip, Joey cleaned out all $3,800 from his savings. In order to have a cushion, Joey swiped one of Teddy's gold Canadian Maple Leaf coins from the yellow rubber duck stashed inside of the toilet tank and sold it to a Cuban antique coin store in town; then, the brothers bicycled to Dan's to pick up the chicken mobile.

In Teddy's workshop, Joey grabbed two down sleeping bags, a pack tent, two inflatable pads, two internal frame packs, two foldable shovels, a fly rod, reel, and ties, portable stove, some gunpowder, duct tape, fuses, Teddy's Infinity metal detector to detect gold, and a big Yeti cooler. Taking their packs inside, they gathered a week's worth of clothes, the Glock, three boxes of bullets, and some hiking shoes. Then, they laid the gear out by the door and left, making two critical stops.

At Gooch's— they picked up ten Nalgene bottles, an extra tent, a double goose down sleeping bag, and a bear box. From there, they went to the grocery and filled the cart with food. They packed everything snug in the car.

They didn't plan on taking Dog, but he was onto them and jumped in the backseat. Cos attempted to leash him, but he leaped into the front seat. After five minutes of chasing him around the car, they threw their hands up in surrender. Cos put his hands on his hips, suggesting to Joey that Dog's gold-sniffing skills might come in handy; Joey thought about it and agreed.

The sound of tires crushing shells grabbed their attention. Joey spotted Belle's red Cherokee coming up the driveway—Teddy had left the gate open. Turning away, he acted uninterested and hurried back inside to get the last couple of bags, hoping she would disappear by the time he returned. She parked and got out, wearing khaki shorts and a golden tank, her red hair pulled tight into a knot. As she approached, she crossed her arms and frowned at Joey, who exited the house carrying the last bag to the trunk.

"Hi Belle." He didn't make eye contact.

"Why haven't you returned my calls?" she said, following him to the car. "What kind of a jerk are you?"

"Look, Cos is going out of town for a few days on a business trip and I got to help him pack, okay?"

She squawked, "A business trip?! Cos works for *Dan's*. What is it, a special assignment to take chicken to the mayor? Do you think *I am stupid*, Joey? Why are you avoiding me?" Cos exited to the barn. Joey continued packing and adjusting the bags in the back.

"I thought we had the most wonderful night of our lives together, but since the storm, you've acted like you don't know me."

He kept going through stuff, zipping and unzipping bags for no reason. She slammed her hand against the side of the car.

"At least look at me! I *demand* an answer."

He turned, and when their eyes connected, he was back in the deep end. The black and blue was gone from her left eye, and the exquisite fibers in her irises were like those rare gemstones he once saw at a cave in Lookout Mountain, Tennessee. She was strong, too, like that mountain, and he could see distant horizons in her eyes, and even feel the wind blow there.

"Listen, Belle. There's an explanation. I just really don't know how to tell you."

"What, do you have a girlfriend? I can handle it. Tell me the truth." She paused. "Do you have a third nipple?" she said, almost making herself laugh. She slightly grinned and he almost did.

"No, there's no other girl."

"What is it, then?" She turned upset again. Joey placed his hand on her arm to comfort her, but she pushed it away. "*Don't* touch me! Tell me why!"

"Look, I really care about you, but we can't be together."

She became angry, "*Why not?* My heart has been breaking over the past week and when I think about you, I can't even breathe," she looked away, sad. "My mother thinks I am having a nervous breakdown from the storm or something because I am acting so weird, and I don't know how to tell her it's just because of some boy." She began to cry. "I don't know how to tell her it's because I am falling in love."

Joey let his guard down. "Belle, stop crying, please. Listen, when I was over at your house after the storm, your father took me in his office and suggested I stay away from you."

"He did *what*?"

"In so many words, he said I wasn't good enough for you, and insulted my family."

She shook her head in disbelief. "Oh my God, I am *so* sorry." Her tone grew empathetic, her voice softening. "As far as I know, he has never done anything like that before. You still should have told me. How does that change anything about the way we feel for each other?"

"It doesn't, but how can we be together if I have to deal with him all the time around us, attacking me, you know? That seems like a serious problem, unless you want to stay away from him, then I am fine."

"He'll get over it. We'll be in California together anyway. I *am* going to Stanford."

"You're going for sure?"

"Yeah, I decided."

Joey glanced off, took a deep breath, and paused. "Belle, you know he said some pretty bad things about Teddy."

"I am sorry, but there's a reason he acted that way. There's something you don't know about me."

"What?"

She paused for a moment, "At Texas, I dated this guy named TJ. He was nice at first, but our senior year, he became very jealous of other guys. One night he kicked me in the stomach because I was talking to a guy friend."

"What a jerk," Joey said. He moved closer and rubbed her arm.

"I know. I broke it off right away. But after that, he wouldn't stop harassing me. He called all the time, threatening me. I told my father and he became furious. Ever since, he's been trying to protect me. He keeps pushing me to date these sons of his friends."

"I am sorry, Belle. I had no idea, but he's making a lot of assumptions about me and my family."

"I know. I should have never told him about TJ kicking me."

He paused. "Look, I want to be with you, but you have to talk to him about this."

"I will, I *promise*." She took out her phone and began dialing.

He stopped her. "Not now." Moving in, he kissed her, and she wrapped her arms around his waist, tugging his body closer. Her heartbeat against his chest and his against hers; she looked down with a smile and he wiped the lingering tear off her face. Then, she turned her blue eyes up at him.

"So I was thinking we might go to a movie tonight, if you're not going with Cos," she smiled.

"A movie? Isn't it still closed?"

"Yep, but they turned the football field into a drive-in, so people can have something fun to do. Tonight, *Star Wars: The Last Jedi* is playing."

"That's awesome."

"You wanna go?" she said and glanced in the car out of the corner of her eye. "My God, there's enough stuff in here for a month at least! Where is Cos going? He's not going to California, is he?"

"Actually, yes ... well, we're—both kind of going."

"*Really?!* You have to take me, then!"

"We can't, Belle. Taking you for a two-week trip to the

High Sierras isn't the best way for me to warm up to your father."

"Take me. *I am going.* He'll never know."

"We'll be gone for two weeks."

"I can say I am going to look at Texas' business school and to see my sister Courtney in Little Rock. We can stop at her place on the way."

"No, Belle."

"I am going and I don't give a *flying pig's ass* what you say." She ran over and got in the backseat like Dog, hunkering down.

Joey opened the car door and grabbed her by the feet, jerking her out and throwing her over his shoulder with a smile. She yelled.

"Come on. You're staying here." Her legs kicked up in the air and she began hitting him on the back, but kept grinning.

"I'll tell Dan y'all are taking the chicken."

"He already knows. I told you, it's a special assignment," he said with a serious tone, while swinging her around.

"That's bull, I know he isn't *letting* y'all take it."

"You *wouldn't.*"

"Oh yes I would!" He set her down. As she backed away, she started to dial the number on the side of the car.

"He's not there right now."

"Yeah, but I *bet* he checks his messages," she sang and waited while it rang.

"No, no! Stop, Belle! I guess it's all right then—you can come." He smiled.

"Yayers!" She jumped on him, wrapping her legs around his waist. "I have to go home to pack and tell my parents I am going to Texas. Can Leslie come too?"

"Cos invited her, but said she wanted to stay home to help with the store."

"Are you kidding, Leslie has to come so I have a girl to play with. Besides, her parents let her do anything she wants."

"Make it quick. We can't lose any more time. It's 11 a.m. already. Be back no later than 12:30."

"We'll be here."

Joey called Teddy, who was out running errands. He answered gleefully, listened carefully to all the boy's plans, thought hard, and wished them good luck and a good trip.

Belle called Courtney in Little Rock and gave her the plan. Courtney agreed, and Belle told her parents. At the thought of Texas over Stanford, Will offered his American Express. She packed her internal frame backpack and picked up her bow and arrows she used for hunting. Then, she called Leslie, who changed her mind about going after Belle enticed her with dreams of California and adventurous days on the open road with the two handsome guys. They met up at Leslie's house. Leslie's hair was knotted in two side ponytails with a yellow bandana tied over the top. She wore linen shorts and a tank, grinning ear to ear with exuberance; she packed and then they headed to the farm.

Cos hugged Leslie; Joey loaded their packs into the car. Belle walked over with a Bear Archery Carnage bow and a set of arrows.

"I told you I bow-hunted."

"Damn, you weren't lying. This might actually come in handy if Ole Saw's kin are around. I'll pack it there for you." He grabbed it and slid in the back. First, he looked at the route on his Ipad Google Maps app. Then, he spread out a roadmap on the chicken's yellow hood and carefully highlighted the group's route. Cos leaned on his forearms and took off his Ray-Bans.

"We'll go up Route 1 to Highway 57 to I-10 and take it all the way to Alabama, where we'll stay with our granddad Jim. In the morning, we'll get on 10 and travel to I-55, taking it north to Jackson, Mississippi. Then we'll jut over to Little Rock, Arkansas."

"Where do we go from there?" Belle asked.

"We'll take I-40 through north Texas to Oklahoma, where we'll stay for one night. Then, we'll head onto Santa Fe to shack up with Uncle Bo, Teddy's brother, then to Las Vegas for a night, and finally to California."

"How long?" Cos asked.

"It'll take five days to get there. Then, I figure three to four days to find the treasure, plus the return. Looking at least twelve days," Joey said.

"Let's get cooking," Cos said.

He got in the backseat next to Belle, who wore blue mirrored gold aviators, and was blowing bubbles and popping them sharply, and had her elbow slung out the window; she looked at him and patted the seat beside her.

"Keep me company, Cos."

"Okay." Cos sat down, grabbing his Panama estancia hat from the back.

"I like that hat."

"Thanks! Gotta dress for the West."

Alive with the momentum and the promise of wealth, Joey maneuvered the chicken out the driveway. They relaxed into the plush seats, which Cos equated to floating on a cloud, but no one else went that far. Dog perched on the armrest between, scanning the road ahead. Joey hit shuffle on his itunes and Jimmy Buffett's "A Pirate Looks at Forty" flowed out. They motored north on Route 1, admiring the ocean view between homes. The AC was no match for the ninety-eight degree weather, so they rolled the windows down. The wind blew their hair back and the sun hugged their arms.

After a while, Route 1 turned inland from the beach, and the landscape changed from low trees, oaks, and sand dunes to pines and grass fields. They followed it until Highway 57, which cut through north central Florida. Horse and dairy farms dominated the landscape and an occasional orange grove spread for acres, imprinting the air with the smell of citrus. A broad wooden stand on the roadside had a big sign above reading in orange letters on a white background:

FLORIDA'S BIGGEST NAVEL ORANGES.

Joey pulled in and Cos and Leslie hopped out to get two netted bags of oranges from an old farmer wearing a straw hat with holes in it. Indigo clouds floated behind the violet sky ahead of them, warning of rain. They distributed the fruit in the car and hit the road again, heading north. When they reached the clouds, a tropical shower fell.

Around Tallahassee, they hit the first sign of hills. They connected to I-10, taking it toward Alabama. Out of the city, the hills dwindled into flat plains; for the next hundred miles, the car and repetitive scenery provided a meditative landscape for good laughs and nonlinear conversations.

When Cos took a turn driving, Joey joined Belle in the backseat and they talked about various subjects together— the arts, politics, old movies—each topic a wormhole to a galaxy of humor and exploration.

The sun faded and the group stopped at a rest area to raid the Yeti for swordfish sandwiches. Joey whipped out the Tabasco sauce, passing it around.

Dusk arrived, and the group piled back into the car, rolling into the darkness. While driving, Cos announced they would be in Pensacola in about an hour and a half, and then it was another hour and a half to Mobile.

Joey gazed out into the darkened roadside while Belle rested her red head on his shoulder; he rubbed his hand through the locks. Leslie slept with her face pushed against the front passenger window, Dog dreaming in her lap.

ABOUT THE AUTHOR

Duke Tate was born in Mississippi where he grew up surrounded by an age-old tradition of storytelling common to the deep South. He currently lives in Southeast Florida where he enjoys fishing, surfing, cooking Asian food and reading.

You can view his YouTube channel here (http://youtube.com/channel/UCPsBoqTpCgHeyYx7fijEYOw) and his author website here: https://www.duketateauthor.com/.

amazon.com/Duke-Tate

goodreads.com/9784192.Duke_Tate

facebook.com/duketateauthor

twitter.com/duke_tate

ALSO BY DUKE TATE

With Ken Tate

The Alchemy of Architecture: Memories and Insights from Ken Tate

The Pearlmakers

Book 2: The Dollarhide Mystery

Book 3: Gold is in the Air

The Pearlmakers: The Trilogy

Big John Series

Big John and the Fortune Teller

My Big Journey

Returning to Freedom: Breaking the Bonds of Chemical Sensitivities and Lyme Disease

Gifts from A Guide: Life Hacks from A Spiritual Teacher

Translations

Gifts from A Guide: Life Hacks from A Spiritual Teacher - Spanish edition

Gifts from A Guide: Life Hacks from A Spiritual Teacher - Dutch edition

Big John and the Fortune Teller - Thai edition

Coming Soon

Ken Tate in Black and White

The Architect

Quantum Healing: A Life Full of Miracles

Made in the USA
Columbia, SC
06 August 2020

15717805R00109